THE ADVENTURES OF Joy Sun Bear
THE BLUE AMBER OF SUMATRA

BOOK 1

by Blanca Carranza and John Lee

illustrations by John Lee

Joy Sun Bear, Inc.

Joy Sun Bear, Inc.

P.O. Box 878

Agoura Hills, California 91376

www.joysunbear.com

This is a work of fiction. Names, characters, places, and incidents either are the products of the author's imagination or are used fictitiously. Any resemblance to actual persons, living or dead, businesses, companies, events, or locales is entirely coincidental.

Illustrations by John Lee

Cover Design by Shearin Lee

Cover Art by John Lee

Edited by Marcy Pusey

Formatted by Shearin Lee and John Lee

First Edition, September 2018

ISBN 978-1-7325951-0-1

Library of Congress Control Number: 2018957874

Printed in the United States of America

I dedicate this book to my husband, Victor, my children, Nataly and Nicolas, and the many children I have inspired and loved.

-B.C.

For my wife, the most inspiring and supportive person to ever enter my life. And for my daughter, who reminds me what a pure heart can accomplish, every day. This story would not be what is without you two. I love you both, now and forever.

-J.L.

We dedicate this book to all those in search of a new home. We hope that you find open hearts, minds, and doors on your journey.

-The Joy Sun Bear family

Acknowledgments

From the bottom of our hearts, we thank all the wonderful family and friends who have supported us on this journey. Your love, encouragement, and faith in our mission made all the difference in the world.

Thank you to our A-Team - you know who you are! Thank you for your patience while we talked about Joy endlessly and your participation in our readings. Thanks for your friendship, support, honesty and enthusiasm, and for pushing us to make this book the best it could be.

Thank you to two special teachers, Mrs. Lund and Mrs. Ewing, for believing in us and encouraging our efforts through this challenging, yet rewarding, process.

A very special thank you goes out to Prof. Américo Mendoza-Mori, Quechua Language Program Coordinator at the University of Pennsylvania. Your expertise and support was critical in the shaping of some of the characters in our story.

Thank you to all of Joy Sun Bear's followers and subscribers! We appreciate your support through the years. Thank you to the MKB community for welcoming us into your supportive multicultural group.

A special thank you goes to the first global educator who welcomed us into her classroom. Mrs. Bronwyn Joyce from Australia is truly an inspiration! She and her students are changing the world. We will never forget your amazing students in 3/4J.

Thank you to the amazing SPS community, our wonderful editor, Marcy Pusey, and launch team for all your feedback, guidance and support. Without you, we wouldn't be where we are today!

CONTINUE JOY'S ADVENTURE AT HOME WITH THESE *FREE* DOWNLOADABLE ACTIVITIES FOR KIDS!

Kids can color, learn more about the characters in this book,
and create their own character they'd like Joy to meet!

Test reading comprehension with our
Crossword Puzzle activity page!

For these activities and more, visit:
joysunbear.com/blue-amber
and register for *free, instant access!*

CONTENTS

CONTENTS

THE ADVENTURES OF Joy Sun Bear THE BLUE AMBER OF SUMATRA

PROLOGUE

HOME

"Tipah!" the mother orangutan called out to her baby, searching around frantically. Behind her, the human machine roared as it tore through their forest home. It was bigger than the local rhino, with four giant wheels and a massive blade on the front. Dark smoke billowed from the back. Nothing could stand in its way.

Branches snapped under the machine's power, piercing the air and echoing off the trees. Fleeing animals flinched at the sharp, irregular sounds.

The orangutan looked around for her baby. "Tipah!" She saw a little ape, but he was too young to be Tipah. His mother scooped him up and ran deeper into the forest. A pair of tapirs squealed at their calf as they all ran from the mechanical terror destroying their home.

A couple of sun bears scrambled from their trees and fled. In the next moment, the machine knocked into the same trees, ripping their roots straight out of the ground.

A lone Sumatran rhino lumbered deeper into the forest with the other animals. The machine drove right through his favorite nesting spot, sending twigs and dirt everywhere.

The mother orangutan spotted Tipah all the way back by the tree they called home. It was the widest tree in that part of the forest, with large roots that twisted around each other. Tipah searched for something inside the roots. The mother orangutan looked up and saw the machine ripping its way through the forest. She ran toward Tipah as fast as she could, yelling to her, "Tipah! What are you doing?"

Tipah looked up with tears in her eyes, but kept feeling between the roots with her hands. "It's around here somewhere, Mama! I don't want to leave it!"

Tipah's mother reached her, grabbing her arm, "There's no time, we have to go!"

Tipah resisted her mother's grasp. "Wait, I'm sure it's right—"

The roaring of the machine interrupted Tipah. It lurched and changed direction, heading straight toward the pair of orangutans. The mother orangutan grabbed Tipah, pulling her close to her body. She twisted and ducked, so her back was to the tree, shielding her baby ape. The machine's engine roared as it slammed into the tree at full speed. With a thunderous "CRACK!" splinters of wood exploded outward.

Tipah cried out, but was silenced by the out-of-control machine and the sound of their tree splitting open.

The machine bounced off the tree and continued its rampage through the forest. Tipah clung to her mother, who ran deeper into the wilderness with the other animals and away from the chaos.

From the safety of the dense forest, the animals watched the machine finish destroying their home. Eventually it became wedged in a ditch and couldn't get out, but by then the damage was done. The humans were already pouring into the forest and beginning to clear out the trees.

Their home was gone.

Sobbing, Tipah asked, "Where do we go now, Mama?"

Her mother couldn't bring herself to say that she didn't know. Instead, all the animals turned and headed away from the only forest they'd ever known.

They had a long trek ahead of them.

SURPRISES

Rainforests are alive, always changing and filled with surprises. But some surprises are bigger than others, and they can change everything.

On one of the largest tropical islands in the world, Sumatra, the lush green rainforest stretched far and wide. Under the thick canopy of leaves, tangled branches and drooping vines, a young sun bear named Joy hid in the shade of a huge fern. The thick canopy let only a few beams of light pass through it, keeping the forest floor covered in shade.

On Joy's chest, his heart-shaped light patch of fur was bright in the shade of the fern. His older sister, Ayu, had not found him yet. Last time they played hide and seek, she caught him as he ran for safety at the home tree. She ran faster than him, so he had learned to hide better than she could, and now they had the same number of wins. Whoever won this game would be the champion!

A few feet away grew a giant red flower, covered in orange spots, called a corpse flower. It smelled like

5

rotten food and all around it hovered buzzing flies who loved the stinky nectar. Joy felt lucky because Mama Bear had told him it's the biggest flower in the world, but only blooms for a few days at a time, and Joy had found one. She also said that when a corpse flower blooms it means change is coming. Joy wasn't sure about that part.

Ayu liked being clean, and the smell of the flower was so terrible that she wouldn't go near it if she didn't have to. Joy planned to sneak away and hide somewhere else when she finally came looking.

Vines hung from nearby branches, winding around a tree trunk. Joy passed the time by trying to follow one vine at a time up the tree with his eyes. Over and under other vines they would go. He'd traced them as far up into the tree as he could before the vine would curve and vanish around the side of the trunk.

Joy listened carefully for his sister. He could hear the breeze rustling the leaves of the trees high in the canopy. The buzzing and crawling sounds of insects sometimes distracted him. He was curious about what kind of bug made each sound. Joy also heard birds up in the trees singing their songs in the bright morning light.

"Joy!" Ayu called. "Come on! We have to get to the Great Big Fig Tree. Mama and Papa expect us to be there."

Ayu wandered just a few strides near the bush. Joy covered his mouth to hide a chuckle. *If I time this right*, Joy thought, *I might get to pounce on her, then I'll win!*

"Where are you?" Ayu called out again.

Joy waited until she turned so her back faced him. He crouched down and got ready.

"Come on, you little stinker! You're going to get us in trouble—"

Joy ran out of the bush. "Surprise!" he yelled as he leapt at his sister. Ayu looked over her shoulder,

7

eyes wide and mouth open in shock. Joy crashed into her and down they went. Ayu landed on her back with an "Oof!" Joy landed on all fours on top of her, his paws covering the flower-shaped light patch of fur on her chest. Thick sun bear fur protected Ayu from the twigs on the ground, and the leaf-covered forest floor cushioned her fall.

"Ugh! Get off of me," Ayu said, rolling until Joy lost his balance and fell over laughing.

"I got you!" Joy said, feeling very proud.

"Yeah, yeah, you got me," Ayu said, rolling her eyes. "I wasn't playing anymore anyway. I told you we need to get going. It's Harvest Day at the Great Big Fig Tree."

Joy rolled his eyes back at her. "Do we have to? I know it's really important to the orangutans. But for us, it's just a lot of sitting around listening to the same history lesson about the tree. And why don't you just call it 'Big Fig' like everyone else?"

"Because sometimes I like saying the whole name," Ayu said.

"You just like to hear yourself talk," Joy teased his sister.

But Joy knew Ayu was right, and together they walked in the direction of Big Fig.

"The Great Big Fig Tree is special, Joy. Strangler fig trees usually destroy the tree they grow on, but Big Fig didn't. The tree underneath and Big Fig grew tall together."

Joy sighed and interrupted, "And they showed each other respect. The tree underneath helped Big Fig reach the sunlight above the canopy. In turn, Big Fig protected the tree underneath from wind. I know the story already. We hear it several times a year, whenever a Harvest Day comes."

Ayu reached over and poked Joy's tummy. "And you enjoy the figs the orangutans share with us every Harvest Day too, huh?"

Joy's eyes wandered off as he imagined a pile of sweet juicy figs. "Oh, yeah," he said with a smile. His long sun bear tongue fell from his mouth, dripping drool. "I can taste them now."

"Then show some respect for the custom, Joy," Ayu said. "It's not a long time and it doesn't take any effort from you. It's important to the orangutans."

"Okay, fine," Joy said. "You're right, I suppose it's not that bad."

Above the two sun bears, a panicked voice cried out, "It's really bad!"

Joy and Ayu looked up to see two orangutans swinging their way through the branches of the trees. Their long orange fur trailed behind them as they traveled. They headed the same direction as the cubs were, toward Big Fig.

"What happened?" one of the orangutans asked the other. Joy and Ayu just watched on in silence.

"I don't know. No one does," said the other orangutan, "but Keliru said it must be a..." the orange ape's explanation trailed off, the sound of her voice lost in the bending branches and rustling leaves.

"What's going on, Ayu?" Joy asked.

"You heard what I did, Joy," Ayu said, "but let's not waste any time finding out. Let's go."

"Okay," Joy said with a grin, stepping around in front of his sister. "I'll race you!" Joy shouted, then took off running.

"Hey you little cheater," Ayu shouted back at him, laughing. Together they dashed in the direction of the Great Big Fig Tree. *What could cause the orangutans to get so riled up?* they wondered.

CURSES

The two sun bear cubs didn't have far to run. They got to the Great Big Fig Tree at the same time, panting and out of breath. They'd seen the tree before, but something about it made it seem bigger every time they saw it. The tree was so massive that if a dozen sun bears hugged it, their paws wouldn't even touch.

Joy liked the way the fig tree's roots twisted and wrapped over and around each other, going up and down. In the few gaps between the roots, he could see the tree underneath. They heard several voices arguing on the other side. Joy looked up, into the branches of Big Fig.

"Ayu, where are all the figs?" Joy asked his sister. "I don't see any."

Ayu looked up and frowned. "I don't know. I don't see a single one," Ayu said. Then she looked down at Joy with the grin of someone who is about to cause trouble and said, "Guess what?"

Joy looked up at her and raised his eyebrow with suspicion. "What?"

Ayu reached out and touched one of Big Fig's great big roots with a single, long claw. "I. Win."

"Oh come on! That's not fair," Joy said, laughing. He playfully pushed his sister and she gently pushed him back.

A harsh, raspy voice interrupted their play fighting, "This pushes the limits of my patience!" Joy and Ayu stopped pushing each other and peeked around the tree. They could see Keliru, the oldest orangutan, and Papa Bear, with his light fur patch in the shape of a smiling sun.

Keliru sat on one of Big Fig's giant, winding roots. He had the largest stomach, which he scratched often. His long orange fur waved in the air when he moved. Keliru had the most massive dark brown cheeks of all the orangutans; that's why the apes listened to him. Spread out on the other roots of Big Fig were the rest of the local orangutans.

Papa Bear stood on two feet, facing Keliru. He was the tallest sun bear and he had the darkest fur. In the bushes surrounding Keliru and Papa Bear, were many other animals. They sat, watched, and whispered to each other. Joy recognized all these animals from the nearby forest.

Joy looked around, squinting his eyes. He noticed that even though the canopy was thinner here around Big Fig, things seemed to be darker than they should be.

Behind Papa Bear, in the shade of a different tree, another group of animals huddled. Joy had never seen any of them before. There were sun bears and orangutans. There was a family of tapir, animals who looked like large pigs with long, flexible noses. There was even a rhinoceros, with tough grayish-brown skin. They all looked exhausted.

Joy looked closer. The adult animals murmured to each other, each of them looking like they could fall asleep at any moment. Even more concerning to Joy were the young animals. Rather than playing or exploring, each one just clung to their parents or stared off in a daze.

Ayu nudged Joy with her elbow and pointed at one side of the gathering of animals. "There's Mama, let's go."

As the brother and sister ran around the crowd toward Mama Bear, Papa Bear spoke in his deep booming voice, "Keliru, you can't be serious."

Keliru sneered, "I most certainly am serious! These outsiders have brought a curse with them. They must leave or they will bring destruction to our home."

Joy stopped. "A curse? What curse?"

"Not now," Ayu whispered, grabbing Joy's arm and pulling him with her, "Come on."

They got to Mama Bear who stood in front of the weary group of animals watching Papa Bear speak. She saw her cubs and smiled wide, scooping them up into her fuzzy arms. She hugged them so tightly, their faces squished against the moon-shaped light fur patch on her chest.

"There you two are. Where have you been?"

"Joy got lost and I had to find him," Ayu said with a smile.

Joy stuck his tongue out at his sister. "I did not. We played hide and seek and she couldn't find me. So I won." Joy smiled to match his sister's.

Mama Bear gave a tiny laugh, "Alright you two, cut it out." She put her arms around both her cubs and they watched Papa and Keliru's discussion together.

"There's no curse Keliru," Papa Bear said. "The humans destroyed their home. They just need a new place to live, that's all."

"And why was their home destroyed? Hm? A curse!" Keliru waved his hands in the air and the other orangutans hooted and hollered a chorus of agreement.

Keliru gave Papa Bear a very serious look, and pointed a shaky brown finger at him. "You listen mister Sun Bear. There is far more to the world than you know. These animals must have gotten too close to the humans. The two-legged monsters used their dark magic to curse them! That's what destroyed their home! And now, if we welcome them here, the destruction will follow. Look up! Gaze upon the Great Big Fig Tree this Harvest Day, and you will find not a single fig.

The curse is already beginning it's devastation on our forest."

"What proof do you have that it's a curse that has made all the figs vanish?" Papa Bear asked.

"Proof? He asks for proof?" Keliru spoke to all the orangutans. Again the group of orange apes made hoots and shouts to show their support of Keliru.

"I have harvested the figs from this tree since I could walk," Keliru said. "So did the apes before me, and the ones before them. Orangutans have banded together to collect the sacred harvest for generations!"

Ayu looked over at Joy, who was mouthing Keliru's words and waving his arms to mimic the old ape. She smacked his tummy and Joy let out a puff of air.

"What?" Joy asked.

"Show respect Joy. The orangutans have shared the harvest for longer than we've been here."

"What do you mean longer than we've been here—" Joy began to ask, but Keliru raised his voice and continued.

"We came today and when I saw the figs missing, I listened to the Great Big Fig Tree, and it spoke to me for the first time." The crowd gasped in unison. "It told me to beware the newcomers. It said the outsiders bring danger! They bring a curse! The figs disappearing was just the first sign. More evil will come to us from the darkest parts of the Spirit World."

"A curse?" Joy said to himself. "Papa says there isn't a curse, but the figs are all gone. So what else could it be? And where is the Spirit World?"

INTRODUCTIONS

Where Keliru didn't offer specifics about the curse, Joy's imagination began creating things a curse might be, and images of them sprang up like weeds in his mind.

Did a curse mean that all the plants would shrivel up? Would the animals of the forest starve?

Or worse. Maybe the curse would start changing the animals. The animals of the forest might start

growing branches out of their fur. Or maybe they would grow mushrooms all over their heads. Maybe everyone would get bee stings on their tongues and they'd only be able to mumble. Or maybe everyone would start smelling like a corpse flower. No one would want to hug or play anymore if everyone smelled like that stinky thing.

Joy's imagination teased and tortured him. After a few minutes, he was wrenched from his daydream when another animal stumbled into him. The two fell over, and Joy looked up to see a young orangutan he'd never met. Still lost in his imagination, a sudden terror filled him as he realized the ape was one of the newcomers.

"GAH! Cursed one!" Joy exclaimed, scrambling backward and climbing on his sister until he was on her head. "Get back," Joy nervously waved a paw at the orangutan, "I don't want to grow mushrooms on my head!" The little ape slowly sat up, her lip quivering as tears formed in her eyes.

Ayu crossed her arms and looked up at Joy, then gave the young orangutan a sympathetic look. "Please forgive my brother, he can be weird."

"Keep her away, sis," Joy whispered into Ayu's ear.

"Joy, you're messing up my flower. Get. Down."

"What about the curse?" Joy asked.

At Joy's mention of the curse, the orangutan burst into tears, sobbing loudly.

Ayu said, through clenched teeth, "There. Is. No. Curse. You were very rude. Now, get down and fix it!"

Joy climbed down off of his sister slowly, still hiding behind her and watching the new orangutan. "There's no curse? Are you sure?"

"Yes I'm sure," Ayu said with her paws on her hips. "They aren't cursed, they're refugees."

The little ape's sobbing slowed as she looked up at Ayu. She sniffed.

"What's a 'refugee'?" Joy asked.

Mama leaned over, "A refugee is someone who had to flee their home because of something dangerous."

"Like them," Ayu said, waving her paw at all the newcomers, "they had to flee because humans cut down their forest."

A sudden clarity came over Joy, and when he thought of how he overreacted, he felt sick to his stomach. His shoulders and his ears drooped.

"We were refugees once," Mama Bear said.

"We were?" Joy asked.

"Yes," Ayu said, "our old forest flooded with a giant wave from the ocean. We had to travel for days before we could find a forest that would welcome us."

"I don't remember that," Joy said.

"You wouldn't, you were just a tiny bear then," Mama said. "I carried you the whole way. Sometimes I'd hold you in my arms and walk on two legs."

Joy took a moment to think about what he'd just heard. He looked down at the ground and slowly walked over to the little orangutan. His paws rubbed together and he felt like he couldn't look up.

"I... I apologize for calling you cursed. That must have hurt your feelings. I didn't want to do that," Joy said.

The little orangutan smiled through her tears. "It's okay," she whispered. "I wasn't trying to scare you."

Joy looked up and gave her a small grin. "I think I scared myself by listening to my imagination. Hi, I'm Joy."

"I'm Tipah," the little ape said, still sniffing now and then. "You climbed your sister really fast."

"Well, I prefer to climb trees, they squirm less," Joy said.

Tipah gave a tiny chuckle, "You're silly. I like being silly, too. But I don't feel very silly today."

"It's the quickest way to have fun," Joy looked at Tipah as if to inspect her. He smiled at her, rubbed his chin, then began measuring her with his paws in the air.

Joy sniffed the air around her. "You don't smell like a corpse flower."

Tipah smelled her arm and looked confused, "Of course I don't, why would I?"

"I'm checking for curses, of course," Joy said, and winked at Tipah. "You're sure you aren't cursed?"

Tipah smiled a little more, "Yup, I'm sure."

"So, you aren't going to start growing branches?" Joy asked, sticking his arms and one leg straight out and spinning in a circle.

Tipah laughed. "What? No, I'm not going to grow branches."

Joy put his paws behind his head and stuck his long claws straight up. "And mushrooms aren't going to pop out of your head?"

Tipah laughed harder. "No! Of course not."

Joy laughed too. A curse? What a silly idea. Tipah was no different from any of the other orangutans. The other animals were no different either, it was just chance that they were born in different forests. Joy gave Tipah a big smile.

"Welcome to our forest Tipah. I hope you can stay," Joy said.

"Thanks, me too! Who is the big grouchy orangutan?" Tipah asked.

"That's Keliru. He's kind of the leader of the orangutans. He's usually grouchy, but with the figs missing, he's extra grouchy."

"Why do you think they're missing?" Tipah asked.

"Well, I thought there was a curse, but now I have no idea," Joy said.

Tipah jumped up and down a few times. "I can't really see over the bushes. Want to climb a tree and get a better look?"

Joy smiled. "I love climbing. Let's go." They ran over to the tree that shaded the refugee animals. They climbed up the tree and found a nice thick branch to sit on. Joy and Tipah talked while the adult animals debated. They began to find they had a lot more in common than they expected.

But high up in the Great Big Fig Tree, a small creature, hidden in the shadows of the canopy, watched them closely. The tiny thing gripped a tail with both paws and twisted it like a towel. It gritted its teeth and growled in frustration. The creature watched Joy and Tipah quickly becoming friends. It did not like the animals trying to be nice when it had worked so hard to cause this chaos in the first place. If it didn't get involved soon, its plans for mischief might fall apart.

TRICKS

The Great Big Fig Tree towered over the arguing animals, growing even higher than the canopy. The higher branches seemed to reach out to the sky. Meanwhile, the lower branches grew out to meet the nearby trees. The merging branches of the canopy created a single layer of green that shaded the ground below.

It was in the canopy's bundle of branches that a small fennec fox snarled as he watched the young sun bear and orangutan. No bigger than Tipah, the fox had tan fur, the color of beach sand, and a bushy tail with a dark brown tip. Giant ears adorned his head, and his small snout was the same dark brown as the tip of his tail. The dark brown of his snout went up to his eyes, where it turned black and circled them like a mask.

"These two. I'll need to do something about this," he shuddered, "friendliness. Ick. But, first," the little fox reached down and plucked a fig from the branch of the Great Big Fig Tree. He held it in the air and tilted his head, looking at it closely.

"It's too bad none of the other animals can see you, little fig," he said. "Well, on second thought..." He licked his snout and popped the fig whole into his mouth. "No, it's not. It's just the way I like it. Oh, if only that fig was as sweet as the misery below," he laughed.

His laugh cut short as he returned his attention to the pair in the tree below. "Now, to business."

The fox rubbed his paws together, then vanished. For just a moment there was a ripple in the air, like when heat rises from a rock on a hot summer day. Then, that too, faded.

On another branch, high up in the same tree where Joy and Tipah sat, perched a yellow crested cockatoo. He'd been singing all morning and was pleasantly snoozing, his eyes only half open.

In a puff of air and swirling shadows, the fox appeared next to the cockatoo. The cockatoo let out a high-pitched squawk of surprise, and molted a dozen feathers at once. As the swirling shadows faded like smoke, the fox scowled at the bird, then wrapped one arm around his head. He held the bird close to him and put the other paw up to his mouth.

"Shh. I didn't realize you were here," the fox whispered. "I don't want to disturb our friends below us yet. So, you're going to be quiet, right?" The fox squinted his eyes and grinned, showing his teeth.

The cockatoo tried to look as small as possible. He folded in the yellow feathers on his head and brought his wings into his body. The bird nodded to the fox slowly.

"Oh, goody," the fox said as he hugged the bird. "I do like it when I find someone to talk to! I'm a trickster, you see, and we don't generally get to speak to other creatures. Well, not while they're still alive anyway."

The cockatoo gulped.

"Now, you don't look like you're from here. You're from another island, aren't you?"

The cockatoo nodded slowly.

"Hm. I'm not from here either, though you've probably guessed that. I suppose you don't see many foxes like me, especially in the trees," the Trickster giggled. "Let me guess, smugglers stole you and you were one of the lucky ones who got away?"

The bird nodded again.

"Ugh, humans. They are annoying. They are fun to play tricks on though," the Trickster laughed quietly. "Why, just yesterday, I was watching a bunch of them working on a farm. You see all these animals below? I'm why they're here—" the Trickster's ears twitched, then one rotated and angled downward.

"Oh! Wait, the little ape is singing my praise now. Let's listen," the Trickster said, still holding the bird as he leaned over. The cockatoo had to lift a foot to stay balanced.

From the branches below, the Trickster could hear the conversation.

"I'm sad that happened to your home Tipah," Joy said.

Tipah frowned, then looked down and wiped new tears from her eyes. "Thanks. I am too. It all happened so fast," Tipah whimpered, "I didn't even get to grab my favorite blue shiny thing."

"Do you want to tell me about it?" Joy asked, placing a paw on Tipah's shoulder.

"Well," Tipah sniffed and took a breath. "We lived near the human farm. Once in a while they would cut down a few trees and make the farm bigger. When they did, the animals would just move farther into the forest. We were always ready though, because it would take them a few days to get started."

"So why was this different?"

"One of their machines just began tearing through the forest, going all over the place," Tipah said.

Joy scowled. "That's not fair! Animals don't go knocking down human homes just because. Why did they do that?" Joy asked.

"I don't know..." Tipah said, shrugging and looking off in the distance..

Above them, the Trickster buried his snout in the feathers of the cockatoo and laughed. The poor bird's eyes were wide in terror.

"I do, I know!" the Trickster said, patting his chest with a paw. "So what I'd wanted to do, you'll like this, was turn into a tiger and chase the humans around. Oh, what a sight that would have been! But, even though I've been around a long, long time, I haven't practiced being a tiger very much. Without a lot of practice, I couldn't have held it long enough to scare them all. There were a lot of humans working on that farm."

The cockatoo tried to slip away during the Trickster's musings. But the Trickster was too quick, and tightened his grip around the bird's neck. The cockatoo gave a choked squawk.

"Hey now! Don't be rude; I'm talking to you," the Trickster sneered. "Where was I? Oh no, you've made me lose my place in the story."

The Trickster's teeth gleamed as he snarled at the cockatoo. The bird gulped and closed his eyes. Was this his end?

ILLUSION

Surprised to still be on the outside of the fox's tummy, the cockatoo opened one eye and peeked. The Trickster stared at him with one eyebrow raised, apparently waiting for an answer. The cockatoo held up a single talon and did his best tiger imitation.

"What?" the Trickster said. "Yes, right, a tiger. Since there were too many humans to become a tiger, I decided to use their machine instead. I picked a bulldozer, slipped inside as a fly, then turned into a human and drove it right into the forest! Oh what a glorious rampage I had. I toppled trees; I tore up roots. Vines caught on the bulldozer and ripped branches right out of the trees, too. In all the chaos and noise I couldn't help but laugh out loud."

The Trickster stared off into nothing. Memories of the fun he'd had destroying the refugees' forest the day before brought a smile to his face.

"When the plantation owner came to look at the damage, I turned into a fly and blinked right behind

him. I gave him the idea to go ahead and clear that whole area of trees."

The cockatoo stared up at the Trickster, clearly confused.

The Trickster gave the bird a flat look. "Blinking, you know. I disappeared and reappeared right behind him. Do try to keep up or you won't be any fun to talk to anymore."

Flexing his paw the Trickster examined the little nails on it. "Anyway, my whisper magic worked like a charm. The plantation owner didn't even know it wasn't his own idea. He spat the order to the workers and made them all cut down that whole section of forest. When the animals fled, I followed them. They were more miserable than the humans and I thought it'd be fun to mix it up a bit.

"By the time the animals made it here it was the middle of the night. They all stopped to rest. That's when I recognized the giant fig tree, the special one these orangutans dote about."

The Trickster grabbed the cockatoo's face with both paws. He looked down his snout at the bird with a toothy grin, and said, "That's when it came to me!"

Returning the cockatoo to a headlock, the Trickster waved his arm in a wide arc, "Inspiration! A magnificent plan to craft my most elaborate trick in a hundred years. An illusion to hide all the figs on the tree.

It took me hours to perfect, winding the spell around the tree. And placing the blame on the new animals, that was pure genius," the Trickster said,

rubbing the back of his paw on his chest. "All it took was whispering in the old ape's ear about a curse while I pretended to be the tree."

The Trickster laughed again. "Oh you should have seen how wide his eyes got. And the way his cheeks jiggled when he got mad, ha! It was perfect."

The Trickster's ears twitched again, "Oh, their conversation continues."

Joy reached over and put his arm around Tipah. "I'm sure that was scary. I'm glad I can be a friend for you now though."

Tipah smiled through watery eyes, "Thanks. It is nice to meet someone new."

The Trickster made choking sounds, "Oh gross, they're being nice."

Tipah looked at Joy's long claws on her shoulder, "Are these how you climb so well?"

Joy pulled his arm back and spread his claws wide, "Yup! I also use them to collect honey. They help open the honeycomb. It's my favorite treat!"

"I've always wanted to try honey," Tipah said, "but there are too many bees." She crossed her arms and flapped her hands in the air like wings. Tipah made a buzzing sound and spun in a circle, catching herself just before losing her balance.

Joy laughed, "Hey, that's a pretty good bee impression. If it weren't for my thick fur they would *bee* a problem for me, too."

The two young animals burst into laughter.

"How did you climb up the tree so fast?" Joy asked.

Tipah grabbed the branch above her and let her other arm hang down. "My arms are really long and strong from holding onto my Mommy so much. And," she said, grabbing the branch with her feet, "my feet can grab like my hands."

"Wow, that's helpful," Joy said. "I wish my feet did that. Or, this would be so fun, I wish my legs were as strong as a tree frog's. Then I could jump from tree to tree!" Joy gave a little jump, but didn't land well. He started to lose his balance, flailing his arms until Tipah grabbed his paw. She helped him get his balance, then they began laughing again.

"Okay, that's enough," the Trickster said. He looked down at the cockatoo and snarled, "I'm going to put a stop to that playtime. You're going to wait right here for me, right friend?"

The cockatoo nodded carefully. The Trickster vanished, and the bird took a deep breath.

Behind Joy, the Trickster reappeared as a tiny buzzing bug inside a little puff of swirling shadow. He got close to Joy's ear, then whispered. His words, carried by his whisper magic, entered Joy's mind.

"She's not really going to be your friend. She's not from here. You can't trust her. She's not going to understand you."

Joy's eyes got wide for a moment and he suddenly stopped laughing. He heard the words, but something about them didn't feel quite right. That doesn't sound like me, he thought, I wonder why I'd think such a silly thing?

Tipah stopped and looked at Joy. "Are you okay, Joy?" she asked.

Joy looked up and smiled, "Yeah, just got distracted."

The Trickster blinked back onto the branch next to the cockatoo, returning to his fox form. The cockatoo squawked in surprise, but didn't move, fearing that the Trickster would eat him. The Trickster huffed and puffed and babbled without making sense.

"How could—"

"But, that's never—"

"Why did—"

"What the—"

"But-but-but—"

"Argh!"

The cockatoo slowly stepped sideways, thinking it was his best chance to escape. When he'd taken a few steps, he turned to fly off, but the Trickster appeared right in front of him. "Abandoning me now? When I could really use a friend? That's not nice."

The Trickster hugged the bird just a little too tightly. "My whisper magic has never failed like that before." The Trickster held the bird out at arm's length. "How could he resist it? How?"

Still holding the bird, the Trickster looked down at Joy with an evil grin. "I guess I'm just going to have to be more... tricky." And one by one, eight more tails appeared, and slowly swished, behind the Trickster.

BRAVERY

The argument between Keliru and Papa Bear continued on in circles, so Tipah and Joy stopped paying attention. The young animals both thought that making a new friend was a better use of their time anyway.

The pair talked about the differences between sun bears and orangutans. Joy showed Tipah how long his tongue could reach. He pinched it between two claws and stretched it out at full length.

"Thee? Ith weawy wong. Ay yewth it to geh bugth ahn honee," Joy said, still holding his tongue.

"Wow, that is really long," Tipah said. Then, from above them, several tiny white feathers drifted down. Joy crossed his eyes looking. The feather landed on his tongue and he sucked it, and the feather, back into his mouth.

"Ack! Gah!" Joy coughed and spat to get the feather out. Tipah covered her face to shield herself from flying sun bear spit.

"I wonder where those feathers came from?" Tipah asked. They looked up, just as a white cockatoo flew between them at full speed.

"Squawk! Squawk!" the bird cried, not stopping to say hi. He flew off as fast as he could, squawking the whole way.

Once the two friends recovered from the surprise, they watched the bird fly away. "I guess he was in a hurry," Tipah said.

Joy laughed, then stopped. He worked his mouth a moment, then spat out the feather. Then they both laughed some more.

Tipah's laugh trailed off, and she frowned as she looked down at the crowd of animals. "If your papa

can't convince Keliru, do you think we'll have to leave?" Tipah asked.

Joy thought about it for a moment. "I hate to say it, but probably. Keliru is the steward of the Great Big Fig Tree. What he wants he usually gets because so many animals need the figs from Harvest Day."

Tipah looked at Joy. "But I don't want to go," she said.

"And I don't want you to either," Joy said. "If anyone can convince Keliru, it's going to be Papa."

Or I could try, Joy heard himself think. His eyes went wide for a moment. Surely Papa could use my help. I could tell Keliru how nice Tipah is, and that they aren't cursed.

Joy smiled. He wasn't used to such bold ideas, but he liked this one. The thought that he could charge in and save the day made him feel strong, and important.

"Wait here, Tipah," Joy said, "I'll be right back."

"Where are you going?" Tipah asked.

"I'm going to help you and the rest of the refugees. Just watch!"

Joy climbed down the tree, ran past Mama and Ayu, and straight into the crowd of animals. He stood up in front of Papa Bear. His throat was tighter than he expected, and he could only just manage to squeak out, "H-Hello?"

Keliru stopped what he was saying and looked down at the little sun bear. His eyes were wide and intense. He scowled at Joy as if Joy had just stepped on his toes.

Papa Bear whispered, "Joy, what are you doing?"

"Yes, cub. What are you doing here, interrupting the discussion of your elders?" Keliru said.

Joy swallowed. He felt like his stomach had dropped into his feet. Suddenly this brave and bold plan of his didn't seem like such a great idea. He rubbed his paws together and forced himself to speak.

"I-I just wanted to say that the refugees aren't cursed. And they aren't bad. I've made a friend with one and she's really nice. Can't they stay?"

Keliru's eyes widened for just a moment. Then he scowled even harder than before. "Absolutely, not!" Keliru shouted. Joy flinched, but kept looking at Keliru. "How dare you associate with the cursed ones. You will be responsible for the curse moving faster than before!" Keliru shouted.

The other orangutans looked confused, but one by one their eyes popped wide open. They frowned and shouted at Joy.

"He's just a cub, what does he know?"

And another, "First it's the figs, then what?"

"We can't trust them!"

"Who knows what they'll do!"

"What if the human monsters followed them here?"

And on and on. The orangutans, and even some animals in the crowd, said every mean and scary thing

they could think of. Joy didn't believe any of it, but
they were all talking so quickly, one after another, that
he couldn't get any words out. They were so loud that
even Papa Bear could barely say anything.

With each animal shouting something at Joy, his
shoulders slumped. He wanted to curl into a ball. The
arguing got even louder than it had been before. Joy
felt a tear come. *It didn't work,* he thought to himself.
*I've let Tipah down. I've made it worse than it was
before.* Joy started crying and ran straight to Papa
Bear.

Papa Bear caught Joy and hugged him tightly. He let Joy cry into his sun-shaped light patch and patted his back. After a moment, Joy looked up at Papa Bear, "I've made it worse Papa," he sobbed, "they're even more angry than before! I was just trying to help."

Papa Bear looked at Joy and gave him a smile, "I'm proud of you Joy. That was a very brave and hard thing to do. They aren't being mean because of you. They're mean because they're scared."

"But it couldn't have been the refugees!" said Joy as his sobbing calmed. "They aren't cursed. They're animals just like us."

"I know Joy. And you're right." Papa Bear rubbed his paw on Joy's head. "For now, why don't you run along, let me finish dealing with this. You tried your best though, and I'm so proud of that."

Joy gave Papa Bear one more hug, then walked back toward the tree where Tipah was.

The Trickster's chest swelled with pride. He had tricked Joy into interrupting the angry orangutan. Then, he had deceived the crowd into crushing Joy's spirit.

"And now," the Trickster said to no one, "it's time for the grand finale."

As Joy sulked back toward his friend, the Trickster turned into a bug and blinked right behind Joy. He took a deep breath, then using his strongest whisper magic, sent his words into Joy's mind.

"I made things worse," he whispered. "She'll never believe I was trying to help. The refugees will have to leave and she's going to blame me. She'll never be my friend."

Joy's eyes popped open and he stopped in his tracks. To Joy, the thoughts that filled his mind felt loud and impossible to ignore. Doubt flooded his heart.

The little sun bear began crying. "I can't face her, she'll never be my friend now." He turned to his right and ran into the forest as fast as he could.

Still in the form of a tiny bug, the Trickster let out a tiny, squeaking laugh. "Oh, that was rich! Worked better than I hoped," he said to himself.

But as he watched Joy run into the forest, his laughter stopped dead. A faint golden glow was coming from a tiny bird that watched Joy. The Trickster knew a magic glow when he saw one.

"No!" the Trickster hissed. "Not another magical creature! It could ruin everything." Joy and the little glowing bird disappeared into the forest.

"I have to see who that is and stop them," the Trickster said. He morphed into a cockatoo and followed them.

LIGHT

As Joy wandered deeper into the forest, the sounds of the animals arguing by Big Fig slowly faded away. He walked for a little while, thinking about how he'd let down his new friend. His feelings distracted him so much that he hardly realized the direction he traveled. Before he knew it, he'd wandered into the darkest part of the forest, where the canopy was thickest.

The Dark Forest, as it was sometimes called, was quieter than other places in the forest. Less light through the canopy meant less plants on the ground. Less shrubbery meant there were fewer small animals scurrying about.

Joy wasn't afraid of the Dark Forest. He'd been curious and visited it before. He knew the way back home if he wanted to head that way. But his heart told him it wasn't time. He still felt afraid that there was no way Tipah would forgive him. Not after he had riled up the orangutans on accident. Now they were even more hostile toward the refugees. What a mess!

Instead, he marched forward. He climbed over winding roots and fallen tree trunks. He ducked under hanging vines. He walked faster and faster, trying to think more about his hike than his mistake from earlier. But the wind passed through the canopy and rustled the leaves, and the sound reminded him of all the chattering orangutans.

Try as he might, Joy's imagination kept finding ways to remind him of how bad he'd made things back home. He climbed over a log, only to have it break underneath him. He said "Hello" to a flying squirrel, and it ran off without replying. Even the squawking birds sounded like they were saying, "Curse! Curse!"

He came upon a yellow spider with black spines on its body. She wove a giant web suspended between two trees. Joy leaned over to get a closer look, being careful not to get too close. He didn't want to ruin all that spider's hard work, too. The spider spun her web in a spiral that grew bigger as she worked. A few drops of morning dew still clung to it, but that didn't slow down the spider at all. She continued to weave and weave, making the web more beautiful with each lap.

"You're lucky, aren't you?" Joy asked. "You don't have to worry about letting anyone down. I wonder if I could turn a bunch of vines into a web and live alone like you?"

The spider completed a lap around her web, closing the spiral. She crawled out onto one of the support threads. Carefully, she dropped down, swinging on a silk strand all the way to the opposite tree.

"Showoff," Joy scoffed. But he smiled then, and said, "Well, I may not be able to do that with a vine, but I bet my new friend Tipah could."

Through the web, something caught Joy's eye. A bird, unlike any bird he'd seen before, flitted a little ways away. It darted back and forth, but seemed to be a bright golden color, and had two long plumes on its tail. It hovered for a moment, and then flew into the bushes.

Joy looked up from the web. He rubbed his eyes with the backs of his paws. He could see no sign of

the bird, but he could hear a familiar buzzing sound coming from the direction he thought the bird had flown. Joy walked around the web and followed the sound.

Joy passed through the bushes the bird had vanished into. Looking around, he spotted the bird looking right at him, then it dashed behind a tree.

"Oh, come on!" Joy whined. He followed the bird, even more quickly this time.

Joy got to the tree and leaned up against it. He peeked around it and found the bird. He could tell the bird glowed with a soft gold light. There isn't enough light to make the bird's feathers shine. *What's going on?* he thought to himself. He slowly approached it, taking one silent step after another, but again the bird zipped away.

Joy gritted his teeth and growled. "I'm just trying to see what you are!"

Again and again Joy would catch up to the bird only to have it vanish before him. He chased the glowing bird deeper and deeper into the forest. Passing through a pair of bushes, he came upon a tiny pond next to a steep slope. On the slope side of the pond was a small waterfall, no taller than an elephant. The canopy had a gap in it above the water, and light poured in from the bright morning sky.

Joy studied the rainbow in the mist from the waterfall. "This is the prettiest thing I've seen all day," he said.

Joy looked around but could not see any sign of the bird. He began to walk around the pond. He noticed how the ferns around the pond grew so big their leaves hung over the water. He couldn't tell what it was, but something about the leaves of one of the ferns looked strange to him.

Joy focused on the strange looking fern. Suddenly, the glowing bird came flying past, right in front of his face! The bird flew straight into the waterfall, making the water glow. The glow traveled up the waterfall and disappeared over the slope's edge.

"A climb? Really?" Joy said. "Ugh, fine."

Joy started climbing the slope. The mist of the waterfall made the roots and dirt wet, and he slipped after only a few feet.

Joy growled at the slope. It wasn't straight up and down, but close. He tried again, stepping on vines and roots to help him climb. He slipped again, tumbling down to the ground. He got up and snarled at the steep slope in front of him.

"It's no use," he whined, "there's no way I'm getting up that."

Then Joy saw golden light reflecting off the leaves of the trees at the top of the slope. Joy looked up and watched the glow move around. He saw how the branches of the canopy reached out to each other, and how vines would stretch from tree to tree.

"Hmm," Joy said, "That gives me an idea."

SPLASH

Joy knew that if he crawled too far out onto a branch, it would snap. From as high up as the branches were, that was going to hurt. But he had a plan.

Joy picked the closest tree and began to climb. He got to the first large branch of the tree and looked around.

"Top of the slope is still too high," Joy said. He climbed higher.

The next branch was a little smaller, but high enough that it was above the top of the slope. Joy also found the other thing he was looking for.

He crawled out onto the branch carefully. It creaked, but didn't bend. Joy reached for the key to his plan, a thick vine that draped over the branch. He grabbed hold of it and traced it with his eyes up and up into the canopy. The vine came from a tree above the slope.

"Well that's lucky," Joy said.

Joy gave the vine a gentle tug. Nothing happened. He tugged a bit harder. Still nothing. He took a deep breath, looked away, and yanked hard on the vine. Joy felt the vine go tight, but nothing else.

"Huh," Joy said, "this might work." He grabbed the vine with both paws. Then he paused, wrapped the vine around himself, and held on tight.

"Here goes nothing," Joy said. "Time to be the spider!"

Joy took a deep breath and took a step, then another, then he jumped toward the slope.

Joy dropped just a little, but the vine went instantly tight.

"Woohoo!" Joy shouted as he swung toward the slope. It worked! It worked! Joy thought.

Joy cleared the top of the slope and kept swinging until he was parallel with the ground, looking up at the canopy. That's when he heard the sound of a branch snapping. "Uh oh," Joy said as the vine went completely loose. He fell straight down, landing flat on his back. The air left his lungs and he laid there stunned, struggling to take a deep breath.

When he finally could inhale again, he whispered, "Owww."

Joy could do nothing. He lay there looking up. He observed that the forest on this side of the pond got more light from between the canopy. There were a few more bushes and the trees were just a little bigger.

When he could finally sit up, Joy did not see any sign of the bird. He crawled a little closer to the waterfall. There Joy took a seat on the thick root of a tree. He leaned against the trunk, his back to the waterfall, slowly stretching.

"That was not my best idea," Joy said to himself. "I really should listen to Mama and think things through more."

Joy closed his eyes and took a moment to enjoy breathing again. He began drifting off to sleep when a familiar buzzing sound started right in front of him.

It was so close, he could feel the vibrating air on his nose. Joy opened his eyes quickly to find the bright, glowing, gold and red bird hovering just in front of his face.

"Gah!" Joy cried, scrambling backwards. His foot caught on a root and he tumbled backwards. His paws flailed about, but he couldn't find anything to grab. Joy fell through the air. He felt mist on his nose and

realized he was dropping right into the pond. He took a deep breath.

Joy hit the water but didn't sink far. Underwater, his body rolled and his head popped up to the surface. Joy flailed his arms about, trying to stay afloat.

"Help! Gah! I can't swim!" he cried. Joy splashed around and coughed water.

"Hey now, it's okay," came a calm voice. "Just put your feet down, it's not that deep."

Joy did as the voice instructed. He put his feet down and, sure enough, he stood up in the water. In fact, the water only came up to his chest. His wet hair hung flat against his body, making him look too thin, and a little pathetic. Joy looked around, but saw no animals except a tree frog perched on a fern leaf over the water. The tree frog was bright green, with a pale brown back and belly. It let out a small, chirping croak.

"That's strange," Joy said out loud. "I wonder who said that?"

The tree frog tilted his head, then said, "Well I did, of course. And a 'Thank you' would be polite."

"Wow, a talking tree frog!" Joy exclaimed. He smiled from ear to ear and moved toward the frog.

"What? You've never spoken to tree frog before?" the frog asked.

"No, I've always wanted to, but they, I mean you, I mean frogs, always jump away instead," Joy said. "I never knew you could talk."

"Oh," the frog said, looking side to side quickly, "well, isn't that interesting."

"It totally is!" Joy said. "Hey, so how far can you jump? How long is your tongue? I've got so many questions! Oh, and thank you too, for helping me not drown."

"You do have a lot of questions," said the frog. "If you don't mind, may I start? What made you think jumping into the pond head first was a good idea?"

Joy looked up at the edge of the waterfall that he fell from. "Wow that actually is kind of high up."

Joy looked back at the frog, "Well, that wasn't what I was trying to do. I..." Joy waited to finish his thought. He realized he didn't know this frog, and if he told him he'd been chasing a glowing bird, the frog might think he was crazy. "I was trying to catch my breath from climbing the hill. Something surprised me and I fell backward, and into the pond. It's been that kind of day, really."

"Oh? Rough day?" the frog said.

"Yeah," Joy climbed out of the water and sat on the edge of the pond on an old fallen tree trunk. The rotting log grew patches of mushrooms, but it still gave

Joy a nice place to sit. "I tried to help a new friend and some other animals, but it didn't go like I wanted. In fact, I think I made things worse."

"That is rough," the frog said. "I tried to help some animals a long time ago. But then I had to leave suddenly, and couldn't go back to finish. I think that only made things worse for them, too. Do you want to tell me about it?"

Joy looked at the frog and smiled. It felt good to have someone to talk to, especially someone who understood how he might feel. "Thanks, that'd be nice. Well, it started this morning..."

After a few minutes, Joy finished his story, "...And that's why I ran off instead of back to my sister and Tipah. I just felt so bad about letting her and all the other refugees down. I wandered until I came here. Thanks for listening."

"Oh no problem at all," said the frog. He grinned slightly and said, "I'm glad you dropped by."

Joy paused for a moment, then realized the joke. He gave a short laugh, "That was good. Tipah would like you too. So what's your story?"

The frog waved a foot as if to shoo off the idea. "That was a long time ago. Like I said, I tried to help some animals but didn't finish. Because of that, I'm afraid they aren't using what I taught them in the right way. Now I'm looking for a way to get back to them and help.

And actually, it's why the refugees are in the situation they're in right now. And if we're not careful, we could lose your forest, too."

QUESTIONS

"What?! Well, you have to go back and fix it!" Joy said.

"It's not that easy to get there from, well, from where I am."

Joy looked down at the ripples in the pond. "I understand. I'm not sure how to go back to before I messed things up either."

The frog surprised Joy with a loud croak. "You did not mess anything up!" he said. "You showed bravery and respect trying to help your friend."

"Thanks," Joy said, "but I didn't convince Keliru and now he is more sure there's a curse than before."

"Bah," the frog scoffed, "curses don't work like that. Even if they did, humans wouldn't be able to do it."

"Hang on," Joy looked suspicious, "are you saying curses are real? How would you know?"

"Oh, I've known a magical creature or two. I'm even friends with some. The world is bigger, and much more amazing, than you realize, little bear."

Joy looked sideways at the frog. "Wait a second. Is one of your friends a little golden bird?"

"Ah, you've met Kinti? Yes, she is a very dear friend. She's a hummingbird, from very far away."

"Well, I didn't meet her. I just... followed her here." Joy hesitated to ask his next question, but decided that if a frog could talk, anything was possible. "So, does she really glow?"

The frog smiled wide, "Yes! You could see that? What color did you see?"

The frog's sudden excitement surprised Joy, but Joy felt relieved to know he was right. "Uh, gold, I think. She moved so fast I could barely tell for sure."

The frog hopped a little closer to Joy on the leaf and smiled, "If you could see her glow, then you have something special in you. After listening to your story, I believe you can still help your friend. And maybe, just maybe, you'll be able to help me too."

"How?" Joy asked.

The frog looked around, then back at Joy. "I have to go soon, this talk took longer than I expected. Listen carefully, Kinti can take you where you need to go. There, you'll need to find something special. Trust yourself, and you'll have what you need to see the solution. Oh, and don't let any humans see Kinti."

"Wait, humans? Why would I need to watch for humans? And what do you mean she can take me where I need to go?" Joy asked the frog. "I mean, it's

61

not like she could carry me, right? Where would I go, anyway? And what am I looking for?"

The frog looked back at Joy, then hopped toward the end of the fern leaf.

"No time for more questions, Joy. You'll know it when you see it." The frog bent its legs to jump.

"Wait, how'd you know my name? What's your name?" Joy asked as quickly as he could.

The frog looked back at Joy, "Viracocha. My name is Viracocha."

"Veer-a-who?"

"Veer-a-koh-cha. Once you've helped your friend," the frog jumped into the air, "come back and tell me all about it!"

With an impossibly tiny splash the frog dove in the water, hardly making any noise at all.

There Joy sat, alone again, on a log next to a pond in the darkest part of the forest. It was quiet. Joy looked around, trying to figure out what to do next. He searched the pond for any sign of where Viracocha went, but could see nothing.

"What a strange name," Joy said. Looking back at the fern, he thought it seemed to be missing the leaf the frog had been sitting on. "Where did that leaf go?"

Before Joy had time to think about it more, he heard that familiar buzzing sound above him. Looking up, he saw the little golden bird fly over the top of the waterfall... and it was flying straight for him.

WONDER

The bird stopped just in front of him. Gold feathers covered her, with red feathers on her head and chest. Her tiny wings moved faster than Joy could see. It was as if she hovered in one place. She had two long tail feathers that ended in little round shapes. Her beak was long, and her tiny feet curled up next to her, surrounded by little tufts of white feathers.

Joy looked at her and she looked right back at him. Since she wasn't darting this way and that, Joy could see that she did glow, just a little. A warm, soft golden light surrounded her. She gave him a tiny tilt of her head, then hummed and made a strange warbling whistle. It reminded Joy of when the wind whipped through the canopy on a stormy day.

"Uh, hi," Joy said, giving her a little wave of his paw. "Are you... Kinti?"

The bird smiled a little, then flew in a small tight circle and let out a high pitched whistle. Joy held out a his paw and Kinti landed on it.

"I'll take that as a 'yes'," Joy said, "after all, you're the only glowing bird I've ever seen. Can't imagine there are very many of you."

Kinti let out a hum that dropped in pitch.

Joy shrugged. "Sure, the tiny frog can talk but not the glowing magical bird. That makes sense."

Kinti gave Joy a flat look and stuck out a long, thin tongue. She made a short buzzing sound, then pulled it back in.

Joy held up his paws, "I'm just saying, it'd be nice if I could understand you a little better."

Kinti flew in a circle around Joy. He held his hands in front of his face, "Hey! What are you doing?" Kinti stopped above Joy's head, grabbed one ear with her feet and gave it a tug.

"Hey cut that out! My sister does that enough already," Joy said. Kinti let go and flew back in front of him.

"I guess you're probably telling me to pay attention, huh?" Joy asked.

Kinti gave a short, high whistle.

"Okay, fine," Joy said, "I'll listen. Can you tell me what the frog meant by 'Kinti can take you where you need to go'?"

Kinti gave Joy another flat look. Her beak drooped just a little.

"Yeah, that's what I thought," Joy said. "Look, it's been nice talking to a frog and meeting you, but this is getting too strange. Even for me. I've already tried to help my friend out once, and I botched it. I don't think trying again with the help of a magical bird that can't give me directions is going to work. I don't need to make things worse for them."

Joy began to turn away, but Kinti made a sharp buzzing sound, then hovered back over the water. She began to glow brighter, and Joy stopped to look at her.

"What are you doing?" Joy asked, but Kinti didn't answer.

Instead, she curled into a ball and glowed so brightly Joy had to cover his eyes with a paw. He opened two claws to look between them though, struggling to see what was happening. In a flash of golden light, the ball grew bigger, and then much bigger. When the light faded, there was no Kinti.

Instead, a big red hot air balloon with a woven basket floated in the air.

"What in the forest?" Joy asked. His eyes felt as wide as a corpse flower, and his mouth hung open. The air balloon hovered over the water, and extended up into the gap in the canopy. Joy looked up and could see the branches of trees bending against the sides of the balloon.

"It's real," Joy said. He looked the balloon up and down. The basket was big enough to fit his whole family. It connected to the balloon by ropes. The ropes attached to gold belts that went around and over the top of the balloon. Where they connected were strange drawings that looked like a sun.

Joy had seen hot air balloons in the distance before. Humans used them to look at things from as high up as birds. He'd never seen one this closely before. "I had no idea these were so large."

The balloon wobbled slightly and hummed.

"Kinti?" Joy asked.

The balloon let out a high whistle and floated closer.

Joy's curiosity overwhelmed his shock. He waited for the basket to get close. The balloon, which was in fact Kinti, stopped just in front of him. Joy reached out with a paw and touched the basket. He grabbed the edge with both paws and pulled down, peering inside. It was empty. He twisted it left and right to look at the sides.

Kinti floated down a few inches until the basket touched the water. She let out a little series of whistles.

"You want me to get in?" Joy asked.

A high whistle came from the basket.

Joy chuckled, "Uh, yeah, about that..."

LEAP

Joy stood on two legs, balancing carefully on the wobbling log beneath him. He held up two paws, and said, "Nope. No way. Not happening."

Kinti let out a strange, low buzzing sound.

"Hey, I'm sorry, but this is all a bit much to take in at once."

Kinti whistled and warbled.

Joy gave the balloon a skeptical look. "I have no idea what you said," Joy said, shrugging, "which is exactly my point. How am I supposed to trust a talking frog that I've never seen before and a bird that can't talk but turns into a human contraption?"

Joy held up a paw to Kinti while his other paw touched around his head. "Maybe I hit my head when I landed up there. Is all this a dream?"

Kinti didn't do anything for a moment, then gave a very short, very low buzzing hum.

"Yeah. Look, you seem like a nice bird...balloon... magic thing? And as curious as I am," Joy said, standing up on his toes to peek inside the basket again, "I just don't think it's the best idea. Besides, I think I've already caused the refugees enough trouble. Keliru thinks there's a curse and bringing more magic creatures isn't going to convince him there isn't one."

Kinti warbled again, this time the end rose up in pitch like a question.

Joy frowned, "I think I should head home now." He turned to leave when a rustling in the bushes caught his attention.

"Viracocha? Is that you?" Joy asked. Kinti made a low humming sound.

Joy stood up again, "Look, thanks for wanting to help me. And I wish I could help you, too. But, I think I've made enough mistakes today. I'm not going to go with Kinti. You'll have to find someone else to help you out."

The bushes rustled some more, and a low growling sound came from within it.

"Wait," Joy said, "frogs don't growl—"

The tiny branches of the bush parted, and the biggest Sumatran tiger Joy ever saw stepped carefully out from the shrubbery. Much bigger than Papa Bear, the male tiger had huge teeth and long, sharp claws. Black fur surrounded his eyes like a mask, and they focused directly at Joy.

Joy gulped. His eyes darted left and right, trying to find a way out. But the tiger charged him at full speed. Joy yelped and tried to stand on his hind legs, spreading his paws to strike at the tiger in defense. But

the trunk under him rolled forward, and Joy tumbled backward toward the pond.

The tiger leapt forward, swiping at Joy with a claw, missing his feet by inches as the sun bear fell through the air. Instead of landing in the water though, Joy landed in Kinti's basket. The balloon scooped Joy up and floated out over the water.

The log continued to roll forward, pinning the tiger's other paw beneath it. The weight of the old tree caught the giant cat off guard and pulled him down, smacking his chin on the log.

"Kinti! Can you get us out of here?" Joy shouted.

Kinti seemed to spit a short buzz out.

The beast curled up, bracing his hind feet against the log and pushing. He pulled his paw free and rolled backward.

Joy looked at the tiger, then up at Kinti. "Okay, it's a deal! I'll go with you and help the frog," Joy shouted.

The tiger recovered, jumped onto the log and used it to spring upward with a roar.

"Just go!" Joy said. Kinti flew upward, pushing against the branches in the canopy.

The tiger reached up to the basket with his two front paws, his giant claws fully extended. Joy ducked

down in the basket and covered his eyes. If he was going to get eaten, he didn't want to watch.

As the razor sharp claws of the tiger reached the basket, a dark, swirling shadow surrounded the giant cat. The shadow seemed to draw in the very light around it, and vanished as quickly as it appeared. When the shadow vanished, there hung the Trickster in his fennec fox shape, flying through the air.

The Trickster's wide eyes watched the red air balloon escape the canopy. As he realized that he'd tried to hold the shape of the tiger for too long, his ears went flat against his head. He fell into the water; his tiny body making barely a splash.

The Trickster popped his head back out of the water, spitting out a stream of it. Water ran off his head, down his ears, and dripped into the pond. The Trickster ground his teeth and watched the balloon drift up, up and away. He let out a groan and grabbed each ear with a paw.

"No, no, no!" the Trickster shouted while he yanked on his ears. "That wasn't supposed to happen! I tried to get that annoying sun bear to run off, not jump into the balloon!"

The Trickster stomped out of the pond onto the shore. He shook off the water and his tail puffed up into a ball.

"What was that bird doing there anyway? And what was that frog?" the Trickster asked himself out loud. "I know the frog sent him somewhere, but where? And why would the bird change into a balloon? They're so slow! Pfft, amateur."

The Trickster took a moment to compose himself. Taking a deep breath, he closed his eyes and grinned. "No matter. I'm sure a falcon can catch up to that balloon, then I'll see what they're up to."

In a puff of shadow, the Trickster transformed from fennec fox to a sleek peregrine falcon. The bird's feathers were smooth, and its claws sharp. It was a bird of prey, made for hunting.

The Trickster took off, flapping his large wings and flying upward in a tight spiral. He cleared the canopy and leveled off. There, in the distance, he could see the balloon.

"Aha!" cheered the Trickster, and with an evil grin he flapped toward the balloon. But a golden aura began to surround the balloon. "What is that balloon doing?" the Trickster said.

The balloon took off like a rocket, zipping over the tops of the trees toward the other side of the forest. The vacuum behind the balloon sucked the leaves right off the canopy.

The Trickster whimpered. His eye twitched as he watched the balloon disappear. "Are you kidding me?" he squealed. He flapped furiously to overtake them. He would end this once and for all.

PERSPECTIVE

Kinti shot through the air faster than any bird in the world could fly. She carved through the sky, zipping around mountains. The wind whistled through her gold belts. Kinti let out excited warbles as she raced through the sky.

The deep blue sky above her was open and filled with light, birds, and just a few clouds. The lush rainforest canopy covered the forest like a blanket under her. Beyond the edge of the forest, right on the horizon, the ocean almost looked like it was breathing.

Joy could see none of the beautiful scenery, however. He'd shut his eyes so tightly even the tiger's claws couldn't have pried them open. Joy had never climbed higher than the canopy, and the idea of being above it terrified him.

Joy had also never been in a storm with wind as strong as what he felt when Kinti bolted through the sky. All four of his legs braced against the basket, and his long claws dug into it to hold him in place. He forgot to close his mouth and his long tongue fell out and flapped in the wind against his cheek.

Joy finally pulled his tongue in and closed his mouth. Between clenched teeth, he said out loud, "What...was...I...thinking?"

But not even a minute later, Joy felt Kinti slow down and then stop. Joy didn't move. He took deep breaths.

Kinti hummed a question.

Between his deep breaths, Joy answered the question he guessed Kinti had asked, "I'm taking deep breaths to stay calm because I'm scared."

Kinti warbled another question.

Joy blew a deep breath out hard. "Because in the last few moments, a tiger nearly ate me, then a magical balloon launched me across the sky! That's why!"

A hum followed by two whistles. Joy realized that Kinti definitely had her own way of speaking; he would just have to figure it out.

"We're-we're safe now, you said?" Joy asked.

Kinti let out a high whistle. Then, she began whistling in a rhythm. Joy realized she was singing, like a bird does. He slowly opened his eyes. From up in the air, the sky was a shade of blue Joy had never seen before.

Peeking over the edge of the basket with one eye, Joy saw how the ocean was a deep blue color, just like the sky. The only reason he could tell them apart was the ocean's sparkling surface. Joy had heard of it, but never seen it himself. The beauty of it lifted his spirit and he smiled. He forgot for a moment that he was nearly eaten just a few deep breaths ago.

"Wow! It's beautiful from up here. And so quiet," Joy said. "I always wondered why birds like to fly. I think I get it now."

Kinti didn't stop singing, but slowly spun in a circle so Joy could see everything. From that high up, Joy could see all the way to the edges of the island. For the first time, he saw the end of the forest and how it blended into flat land. He saw some human buildings far away.

Joy took a deep breath and peaked over the side, looking straight down. The world seemed to spin around him and he felt his stomach sink. He shut his eyes but didn't pull his head back. Instead he took a deep breath.

Kinti let out a hum that sounded like concern. "It's okay," Joy said, "I just need a moment to get used to it." He gave a short laugh, "I felt this the first time I tried to climb a tree. It will go away." He breathed deeply a few more times, then slowly opened one eye.

The feeling passed and he took in the view below them. Joy could see where the forest blended into wide open grasslands. He could also see where the forest suddenly stopped in an unnatural straight line. On the other side of that line, a long patch of brown dirt.

Joy's grip on the basket got tighter. "Kinti, are those brown patches where the humans cut down trees?" he asked. He thought of how scary that must have been for his friend and the other refugees.

Kinti let out a short warble. Joy realized that he had no idea what she meant, but it sounded high pitched, so he guessed it was a "yes."

"I didn't want to be here right now, Kinti. But, we made a deal. And, to be honest, once I got over the horror, the ride was kind of fun."

Joy sat down in the basket, leaning against the side. "But, what if I mess this up? What if I can't find what Viracocha wanted me to find? I mean, he didn't even tell me what it was. And then there's you. How am I supposed to keep you hidden? Can you change back into a bird?

"I couldn't convince Keliru not to hate the refugees, what am I supposed to do when a bunch of humans are around? Tall, scary humans who cut down trees for fun and do...do...I don't even know what they might do to an animal like you or me!"

Kinti didn't say anything. Instead, she gently floated downward. She reached the forest, hovering just above the ground in a small clearing.

"What am I doing here?" Joy asked himself out loud. He felt the basket tip. "Kinti? What are you—" he began sliding on his butt toward the other side of the basket.

Just before Joy bumped into the other side, the basket glowed bright gold and morphed back into a hummingbird. Kinti timed her change just right, and Joy slid through empty air for a moment before his feet touched the ground.

The momentum made Joy take a few steps. Kinti flew down in front of him, whistled and flew forward.

"Hey, nice trick. Wait for me, I'm coming," Joy said, following Kinti into the forest.

"Where are we going anyway, Kinti?" Joy asked. Kinti led him through the forest, humming and whistling a story. Joy didn't understand any of it, but followed her anyway.

"I guess I'm going to have to trust you. You're my ride back after all. Hey, Kinti?"

Kinti stopped and looked at Joy.

"Thanks for saving me from the tiger," Joy said.

Kinti smiled and buzzed, then she dashed into a fern.

Joy pushed through that fern and reached the edge of the forest. He left the shade of the canopy and entered a wide clearing. Joy had to cover his eyes with a paw to keep the high midday sun from blinding him.

When his eyes got used to the light, his heart sank. He stared out at dozens of tree stumps. Sawdust littered the ground. The stumps were the only sign that a forest had grown here. Only one tree remained, standing tall on the other side of a stack of logs.

The humans had brought in machines, leaving large grooves in the dirt behind them.

Joy looked at the stack of logs, trees that no animal would be able to climb again. "Kinti," Joy said, "those were trees yesterday. I had no idea it was this bad."

He stood there for a moment, at the edge of the clearing. A clearing that hadn't been there a couple of days before. It had been a forest, full of animals and plants, bugs and birds. Joy began to feel angry.

"The humans are monsters," he growled. "And I'm going to do something about it."

SNEAKY

I knew what happened," Joy said, "Tipah told me the story, and I had a picture in my head. But seeing it up close, that's different. I couldn't have imagined this even if I tried."

Kinti flew up and perched on Joy's shoulder. He looked over at her. "Do you think Viracocha was right? Do you think I'll find a way to help Tipah here?"

The tiny golden bird smiled, closed her eyes, and gave Joy a big strong nod of her head.

"Then let's do it. I can't do nothing, not after what I messed up. And not after seeing this. If I can make something good happen, I should. Right, Kinti?"

Kinti trilled and her wings flapped so fast they seemed to disappear.

"Now," Joy said, looking out at the clearing, "where do I start?"

A giant tree stump, bigger than any of the others, sat alone in the middle of the clearing. Joy remembered how Tipah described her home and realized that must be it. Behind the grass at the bottom of the stump, something sparkled, grabbing Joy's attention.

"Hmm, maybe there?" Joy said.

He looked around. He could see humans on the other side of the clearing, which was uphill a bit and closer to the farm. Some talked to each other while others ate food. Some sat on benches and some stood up or squatted on the ground. Joy thought of how long it took Papa Bear to finish a meal.

"We don't have long, Kinti," Joy said, "but now is our chance. Stay close."

Kinti dove into the fur on Joy's shoulder and clung to it with her tiny feet. Joy stayed low, and on all fours he crawled toward the big stump. Kinti whistled a quiet question.

"Just like hide and seek, Joy," Joy said, then gulped. "Just with scary humans, extreme danger, and the safety of the refugees and your forest at stake. No pressure."

From one stump to another, Joy crawled, dashed, and hid. He was halfway across the clearing when one of the human machines rolled up to the big stump of Tipah's old home and stopped. It was loud, rumbling, and sounded like Papa Bear when he snored. Joy ducked down behind a small stump and peeked over it.

The human riding the machine reached down and did something. The rumbling noise, and the smoke from behind it, stopped. He grabbed a small bag and climbed out of the machine. He took a couple steps and the machine began to roll forward slowly.

The human yelped and ran back to the machine. He threw his bag onto the step and jumped back in. He slammed his foot on something, making a loud grinding sound, and the machine stopped. The human jumped off and walked around to the other side of the machine. Joy couldn't see what he did, but after a moment he walked back to the humans on the other side of the clearing.

Joy waited to be sure it was clear, then he continued sneaking to the giant stump. He moved the branches and leaves around the stump looking for the sparkle that had drawn him there in the first place. The burning smell of the machine next to him made him gag and cough. He did his best to ignore it and focused on his search.

"Kinti, I know I saw something," Joy said. "Aha, there!"

Tucked inside a tangled group of the tree's roots, Joy found it. A small blue stone, just a tiny bit bigger than a fig and shaped like a long egg, gleaming in the bright sunlight. While mostly smooth, it did have one side that had jagged edges, like it used to be part of another, bigger stone. The stone looked solid, but Joy saw swirling brown shapes, like clouds frozen in time, inside it.

"This must be Tipah's favorite shiny thing!" Joy said. "She'll be so happy if I can bring it back to her."

Kinti let out a long hum, her eyes nearly as wide as Joy's. Joy reached down inside, between the winding roots, to grab the stone. He stuck half his arm into the tangle of roots, but he could just barely touch it with his claws. As nimble as his long claws were, they were no match for an orangutan's fingers. After a few tries, he finally got a grip on it.

"Got it!" Joy yanked his arm out from under the roots. But space between the roots was narrow, and Joy held the stone at the wrong angle. The stone got

85

stuck and popped out of Joy's grasp, falling deeper into the gap between the roots.

"Oh come on!" Joy growled. He held his eye up to the hole. "I can see it Kinti, but I'm not sure if I can reach it."

Kinti flew off his shoulder and into the hole, lighting it up with her glow.

"Thanks Kinti, but I can't look and reach for it at the same time," Joy stuck his paw in again, feeling around for the stone.

Kinti buzzed and whistled, warbled and hummed.

"Ugh, Kinti, I know you're trying to help," Joy said, "but I can't understand your directions." Joy stretched more, felt the stone, and grabbed hold of it. "Yes!"

Kinti gave a low whistle. "Yeah, I know," Joy said, "carefully this time."

Joy slowly lifted his arm, but then he heard something. "Kinti, what's that sound?" Joy whispered. But he didn't need her answer. He realized he was hearing human voices, and they were getting closer.

Every instinct Joy had told him to run, to drop the stone, and head straight for the forest. No! Joy thought, I've come this far, I'm not leaving without that shiny rock!

From under the machine, Joy saw human feet approaching. Joy held his breath and focused on slowly pulling the stone out from under the tangle of roots.

The humans split up, one walking one way around the machine, the other going the other way. Joy turned the stone, gripping it tightly so he didn't lose it again. The stone came free, and Joy dashed for the only hiding spot he could see, the space under the machine. He got low and crawled under it into the shade of the giant human contraption as the two humans walked past the stump. They met again and faced the giant stump of Tipah's old home tree. They talked back and forth, pointing at the tree stump. Joy closed his eyes and let out a quiet sigh of relief.

"That was close, Kinti," Joy whispered. "Kinti?" He looked around, but did not see the bird.

Joy looked back at the stump. There, tangled in the roots that had held the stone, Kinti looked back at him and trembled.

87

DISCOVERY

The big human machine Joy huddled under gave off a stench that was beyond words. The pair of humans stood between him and the stump of Tipah's old home tree. Their height surprised Joy. If he stretched up on two feet, his head would just barely be higher than the human's knees. Kinti looked at Joy with impatience, and Joy looked back with confusion.

"What do I do? What do I do?" Joy whispered to himself. "Okay, it's okay. As long as Kinti stays under those roots, the humans won't see her. She'll be fine, and they'll leave, and then we will be able to leave together."

One of the humans turned around and walked up to the machine. Joy backed up and scooted over behind one of the giant tires. He heard the human open something, then a thick metal chain dropped to the ground next to the tire.

The human walked around the tree, dragging one end of the chain with him. Joy peeked around the wheel carefully. The human wove the chain in and out of the roots of the tree.

"Oh no," Joy said to himself, "oh no, oh no! If he gets all the way around the tree, he'll see Kinti."

Joy held the blue stone to his chest. His heart pounded and he took shallow, panicked breaths.

"What do I do? I've messed things up again! I didn't even want to be here. I just wanted to fix things at home. I just want to fix things now."

Joy closed his eyes tightly. "I just want to know what I can do!" he said to himself.

In his paw, he felt the stone getting warm. "Huh?" Joy opened his eyes to look down. Inside the stone, the

little cloud-like shapes glowed with a warm, golden light. Sparks of light floated and zipped from the stone, landing in the hairs of the heart-shaped light patch of fur on his chest. The heart patch began to glow, then a burst of light shot out of it.

Joy slammed his eyes shut again to block out the light. When he did, he felt very strange inside, like being pulled by the scruff of his neck up, up, up. He felt like his feet were leaving the ground, but he knew that under the machine he had nowhere to go.

The feeling only lasted a moment. In the very next, his mind floated out of his body. Joy saw himself frozen in time, eyes shut tight and the stone held firmly against his chest. He looked around and realized nothing was moving. And, everything was gray, he could see no colors at all.

"Whoa," Joy said. He lifted his paws to look at them. They were see-through, and Joy could see himself, through his paws. "Why can I see through my paws? And why am I looking at myself?" Joy said. His voice echoed and sounded strange to him though, like he was alone in a small cave. "I should probably be freaking out," Joy said, "why do I feel so calm?"

Joy looked over at the humans. They stood perfectly still, and did not seem to even be breathing. See-through Joy crawled out from under the machine. The humans stood impossibly still. One wrapped the chain around the tree stump while the closer one bent over, trying to untangle the chain. The chain floated in the air looking like a snake that should be falling, but wasn't.

Joy slowly approached the closest human. As he moved, Joy realized that he wasn't touching anything. He didn't walk, but floated.

The human didn't even flinch at Joy's sudden appearance. Joy waved a hand in front of the human's face, but did not see even a trace of a reaction. He reached out to touch the human, but Joy's see-through paw passed right through the human's arm.

"Huh, that's odd," Joy said. He covered his mouth quickly, then remembered that the humans were frozen. Joy didn't think they could see him.

Joy looked around. The clearing spread out wider than Joy had realized before, and was bright from the shine of the midday sun. But when Joy tried to look past the trees at the edge of the clearing, he couldn't see beyond them. Instead, everything seemed to get fuzzy and wavy, then become unclear. Even when he looked up, Joy couldn't see the sky or the sun. The same strange fog seemed to form a dome around the clearing. The birds in the sky were frozen in place too, just like the humans and Kinti.

"Oh, Kinti!" Joy said, then looked down into the hole where Kinti hid. She tucked herself as far back into the roots as she could go. Even though everything was gray and colorless, Joy saw Kinti's glow even more brightly than before.

Joy looked over the tree stump. If the other human kept weaving the chain through the roots, he would definitely see Kinti soon.

"I have to think of something, and fast," Joy thought. He turned and saw the machine. On the side, human words called the machine a "bulldozer."

"I can understand the human writing? Oh boy, this is getting weirder every moment. That frog has some explaining to do," Joy said.

See-through Joy floated over the bulldozer. He spotted a pedal the human had pushed to stop the bulldozer earlier. On it a label read, "parking brake." Above it, a handle had the words, "Pull to release."

"That's it!" Joy said. He floated back under the bulldozer and up to Frozen Joy.

"Okay, so how do I get back in my body?" Joy asked. Without thinking, he reached out and touched his heart patch. Everything went black, and Joy felt a strange pulling sensation, like falling out of a tree.

Joy opened his eyes and realized he was back in his body. He could hear the humans moving again. "That was so weird," he said, "but I'll deal with weird later. Right now, it's time to save Kinti!"

ACTION

Joy peeked out from under the bulldozer to see what the humans were doing. He was glad to see they were right where he'd just seen them in his out-of-body moment. That meant he wasn't going crazy.

Except now they were moving again. One human unraveled the chain by the bulldozer while the other wound the chain around the roots of the tree stump. He was more than halfway around the tree.

"No time to wait, I have to move now," Joy whispered to himself. He snuck out the other side of the bulldozer and began to climb on top of it. Staying as low as he could, he crawled along the floor to the pedal he'd seen in his out-of-body moment.

When he looked up at the handle above it, he could still read the words, which surprised him.

"Pull to release," Joy said, "well, worth a try." He reached up with a paw and grabbed the handle. He gave it a tug, but it only moved a little. Nothing happened.

Joy moved in front of the handle to get better leverage. As he braced his back feet so that he could

94

pull harder, his left foot bumped into something soft. Joy looked down to see a small bag fall off the bulldozer to the ground.

The bag hit the ground with a soft thud. Joy didn't know if he should get out of sight or freeze and not make a sound. He froze in place, too scared to do anything else. The human untangling the chain looked behind him at the bag on the ground, shrugged, and went back to what he was doing.

Joy let out a sigh of relief. He grabbed the handle more tightly and braced himself, then looked down at the humans again.

They're making a lot of noise with the chain, Joy thought, I hope they don't notice me do this.

He gave the handle a tug. He felt it get tighter, but he pushed his feet down and pulled with his whole body. Then, suddenly, there was a loud pop and a hiss. Joy didn't wait to see if the humans noticed, he dashed off the bulldozer the way he came, jumping to the ground. He landed on the ground and scrambled up to hide behind the giant back wheel of the bulldozer.

The bulldozer did nothing, but Joy could hear the chain stop rattling.

"Did you hear something?" one of the men asked.

Joy's eyes grew as big as the tire he was hiding behind. I can understand them? Since when? How?"

"Don't waste my time," the other said, "I'm almost done wrapping the chain. Hey, did you knock down my lunch bag?"

Just then, the bulldozer began to roll forward. Slowly at first, but then faster and faster.

"Oh no, not again!" one of the humans yelled. The bulldozer rolled down the slight hill the clearing was on, toward the forest.

Joy had curled into a ball to try and be as small as possible. As the bulldozer rolled away, he was afraid that the humans would spot him. Instead, they chased after the bulldozer, and left Joy unnoticed. He peeked around carefully, and when he was sure that both humans ran off, he raced over to Kinti.

"Kinti, are you alright?" Joy asked.

Kinti's eyes were wide and she was breathing quickly, but she nodded.

"Come on, let's go."

Kinti shook her head. She pointed a wing toward the humans, then covered her eyes with the tips of her wings.

"Oh that's right. Viracocha said I'd have to keep you hidden. How am I supposed to do that?" Joy asked.

Then he remembered the bag. Joy turned around and grabbed it, opening the flap and holding the bag open for Kinti.

"How's this?"

Kinti smiled, then darted into the bag. Joy put the shiny blue stone inside too, then put the flap and the strap over his head. The strap rested nicely on his shoulder, the bag bouncing against his hip. He moved around the tree stump and crouched low.

"What do I do now?" he wondered out loud. Joy heard a whistle and looked up. The humans were getting up from their meals.

"Oh no," Joy said. He looked around for somewhere to hide. The closest forest edge had two humans and a runaway bulldozer in front of it. The only other hiding spot he could see was the last tree in the clearing. Joy ran for it, staying as low as he could.

Joy reached the tree and climbed up. He heard Kinti whistle a question from inside the bag.

"Don't worry Kinti. Up in the trees is where I always feel the safest."

Joy climbed up into the thickest branches of the tree. He stopped for a moment, closing his eyes and taking a deep breath. Next to him, he heard a tiny little squeak.

Looking down, Joy saw a baby squirrel. Her fur color matched her big black eyes, which stared up

at him as she held a tiny, puffy tail in her paws. Her tummy was the color of the branch she stood on.

"Oh, hello," Joy said. He stepped carefully out onto the branch where the squirrel was. "Are you alone up here?"

The squirrel nodded, then began to chitter nervously. She pointed across the clearing toward the forest. Joy looked out to the trees and saw a group of squirrels in a tree right at the edge of the forest.

"Is that your family?" Joy asked.

The baby squirrel nodded slowly. She held out her tiny arms and shook her head.

"Oh, you were too small to make the jump with them, huh?" Joy asked.

She nodded, then chittered some more.

"Don't worry," Joy said, holding out a paw, "I'll help you. I'm trying to get to the forest anyway, so I'll take you with me."

The baby squirrel's eyes lit up and she smiled. She darted up Joy's arm and perched on his shoulder, nuzzling her fuzzy head into the hair at his neck.

Joy laughed, "That tickles!"

Suddenly, a terrible sound split the air. To Joy, it sounded like thunder, followed by the loudest, meanest growl he'd ever heard. Joy looked down to see a human at the bottom of the tree. He was wearing something on his face, and in his hands was a tiny machine that looked like a long arm covered in spinning claws. The human raised the little machine up and touched it to the tree that Joy was hiding in. It tore into the trunk, tearing thousands of tiny pieces from the tree.

The little squirrel squeaked in terror and held onto Joy's fur tightly. She chittered quickly and pointed at the stack of tree trunks, then at the human below them.

Joy realized what was about to happen. "Oh no," he said, "that's not good."

FAITH

The human turned on his hand-held tree-cutting machine and shattered the peaceful silence of the forest. The sound of it tearing into the trunk of the tree Joy hid in was like a hundred roaring tigers. It echoed off the trees around them. The branches of the tree wiggled as if there was an earthquake. Joy dug his claws into the trunk of the tree to stay balanced. The tiny baby squirrel dug her little claws into Joy's fur.

Joy couldn't think straight. The shaking tree made it too difficult to focus on anything. He felt the bag press against his leg, and he remembered the stone. Joy reached into the bag and grabbed the stone in his paw. He heard a loud crack, and the tree began to tilt. Joy closed his eyes tightly and tried to focus on the warm stone.

Then it happened. Joy floated outside of himself again, and everything was gray and colorless. Leaves that had shaken loose from the tree hung in mid-air, frozen like everything else. Joy looked at himself. His heart patch was glowing and so was the inside of the bag on his hip. The fur at Joy's neck covered the baby squirrel.

Joy looked down and realized he was floating in mid-air with the leaves. He saw the human on the ground, and the machine he held against the tree. The tree was starting to fall.

"I need a closer look," Joy said to himself. He floated down to the ground next to the human. On the machine, Joy saw new words.

"Chainsaw," Joy said out loud. He looked at the tree where the chainsaw was ripping into the trunk. "That's terrible, even I don't do that much damage

when I'm getting insects. Though, I have to admit, this would make getting lunch easier."

Beyond the tree, Joy saw the stack of logs. Next to it, there was a pile of shrubbery and branches.

"I hadn't noticed that before," Joy said. He floated over to it. It was mostly bushes, ferns, and leafy branches from trees. He looked over at the tree and how it was falling.

"It's not going to land right on it, but next to it," Joy said. Floating up into the tree, Joy looked past his body and down to the ground.

"It's a big jump," he said. "But if I time it right, I might make it into the pile instead of riding this tree right into the ground.

Joy rubbed his see-through paws together. "What should I do? It's a really big jump," he said.

A flicker caught Joy's eye and he looked at it. Inside his bag, the glow from the stone was dimming. Joy felt the magic of the stone pulling him back into his body.

"Wait! Not now!" he said. Joy kicked his legs and flailed his arms trying to get away from himself, but it didn't work. "I haven't figured out what to do yet!"

As the glow dimmed, Joy felt the pull get stronger. Suddenly the sound of the chainsaw came back, and Joy's eyes opened. He was back in his body, and the tree was starting to lean farther over.

"Brace yourselves," Joy warned his tiny friends, and he let go of the trunk and ran toward the end of the branch. The little squirrel crawled under Joy's jaw.

The tree trunk gave one last crack and began to fall. Joy took a couple more steps on the branch, then jumped off into the sky. The bag came off his shoulder and fell through the air in front of him. Joy turned his body so his back was toward the ground. The baby squirrel held onto his fur with two tiny paws, her back feet and tail trailing behind them through the air.

Joy's back hit the pile of vegetation as the tree hit the ground with "crunch". He sank right into it, while the bag with Kinti inside landed on the side of the pile and slid off. Joy felt branches he didn't realize were there break underneath him, but mostly he felt cushioned by all the leaves. He sank only a few feet into the pile, but didn't feel hurt. Joy looked down at the baby squirrel clinging to his heart patch. She held her tiny eyes shut tight and her tail curled around her.

"Hey there," Joy said softly, "you're safe now."

The baby squirrel opened her eyes slowly and looked around. She squeaked and smiled, hugged Joy, then jumped up to the top of the pile. She stopped, waved goodbye to Joy, then dashed toward the forest and her family.

"My turn," Joy said, and he began to scramble out of the pile. But something shifted and Joy's back foot slipped, sinking into the leaves. A branch beneath him trapped his foot and he couldn't pull it back up.

Joy heard someone coming, and he scrambled to try and climb out faster. The more he tried, the more he seemed to get stuck. He could hear a human's footsteps, and his heart began racing. Joy clawed and kicked at the leaves and ferns, but nothing gave him enough leverage to get unstuck.

A shadow appeared over him, and Joy looked up to see a human looming above him. In his hand, the human held a small device that blew fire. Joy tried to read it, but the sun in the sky made it hard to look up.

"Well, well, well" the human said, "What do we have here?"

STUCK

Joy pulled his leg harder, but it only seemed to make his foot more stuck. The human standing above him held up his tiny fire device.

This is it, Joy thought, I'm doomed. He's going to eat me.

The human reached up and turned something on the little device. The flame stopped.

"I'm supposed to burn this pile of leaves and branches," he said, "but it's not supposed to have a sun bear in it." The human laughed, and set down the device. Joy froze.

The human stood back up and started moving big fern leaves and branches out of his way. Joy saw the human trying to get closer and started kicking again, trying to get free.

The human stopped, holding up his hands. "Whoa there, I'm not here to hurt you." He backed up. "Let's see if I can help you out without getting too close. You've got some long claws there, I'd hate to see what those would do to my shirt."

Joy held still again. He wasn't sure what the human was doing, but he was glad the human didn't seem interested in eating him.

"Ah, found it," the human said. "Your foot got stuck in there pretty good didn't it? Here, I'll get you out."

The human grabbed the end of a branch and pulled it. Joy felt it tug on the stuck foot. He yelped a little.

"It's okay," the human said, "I've got you." The human put a foot into the pile and Joy felt it press on his leg. Then Joy's leg was free. He scrambled out of the pile and onto the ground. Stopping to turn and look for the bag, Joy grabbed its strap with his teeth and looked at the human.

The human looked around, then squatted down to look at Joy. He smiled, and said, "Hey, see? You're free. Now look, you're not supposed to be here. We thought all the animals had run off yesterday. I'm sorry we cut

down so much of your forest. Things kind of got out of control, I guess."

Joy paused, looking at the human carefully. He doesn't look so scary now, Joy thought.

"I like the forest, really. Especially that big tree over there," the human pointed at the stump of Tipah's old home, "that one was my favorite. But, the boss said cut it all down, and without this job I can't feed my family, so I had to."

Joy thought about Keliru and how the animals listen to him because he controls the figs. He felt a bit sad for the human.

There were sounds of other human voices getting closer. The human in front of Joy looked behind him, then back at Joy. "You need to go," he said, waving the back of his hand at Joy, "Go on! There's no forest for you here now, go somewhere else where you're safer."

Joy grunted, then ran off into the forest on all four legs, still carrying the bag in his mouth.

Behind him, Joy could hear someone ask about a missing lunch bag. The human who had helped Joy replied, "Maybe an animal grabbed it and ran off?"

Joy made it to the forest's edge without any trouble. Once he'd disappeared into the trees he stood up on two feet and put the bag around his shoulder. Joy opened the bag and looked in.

"Kinti?" Joy said, "Are you okay in there?"

Inside the satchel, a paper bag holding some squishy human food cradled Kinti. She had stuffed her

108

beak deep inside a box of something that smelled like fruit but sloshed like water. On her face was a look of pure happiness. Next to her, a handful of figs tucked in the corner gave off the sweet smell of ripe fruit. Joy tried to remember the last time he had figs, and he worried that Big Fig would never make them again.

Joy smiled. "Well, I'm glad you found something to eat." Joy's stomach growled. He saw a little piece of paper. Pulling it out with his claws, he read it out loud.

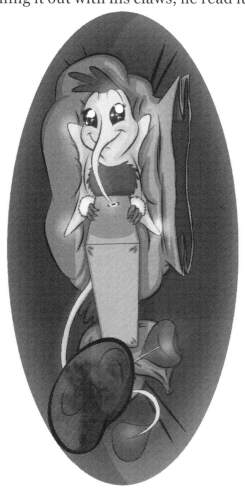

"Damar's take out. Gomak noodles with leeks and ginger," Joy said. He stuck his nose in the bag and sniffed. "Kinti, smells like that's what you're sitting on."

Kinti finished the box of juice with a loud slurp. She pulled her beak out and flew out of the bag, shaking her tail feathers and spreading them out.

Joy reached in and pulled out the shiny blue stone. Holding the stone up between two claws, he looked closely. The glowing golden clouds were turning back into a dull brown, and the stone felt cool again in his paw.

"Kinti, you wouldn't believe what I was able to do with this stone."

The hummingbird warbled a question.

"It was amazing, like I was myself, but not in my body. And then I could understand the humans, and now I can read their words!"

Kinti whistled and hummed. Joy didn't know what she meant so he continued. "This has to be what Viracocha said I'd have to find. But how did he know? And what am I supposed to do with it to help my friend?"

Kinti shrugged her wings and gave a short buzz.

"Yeah, I don't buy it," Joy said, looking at Kinti with a suspicious sideways glance. "You know more, you just can't tell me."

Kinti looked up and sideways and slowly turned around and started flying away.

"Anyway, can you change yet?" Joy asked.

Kinti landed on Joy's shoulder and gave a low, flat sounding buzz. She pointed back in the direction of the clearing with a wing, then brought the tips of her wings close together.

"Still too close to the humans?" Joy asked. Kinti nodded.

"Okay, guess we have a bit of a walk then," Joy said. Together they began walking back toward where they had arrived.

Above them in the trees, a long, dark shape slithered from branch to branch. It followed them, flicking out a forked tongue as it stalked the little sun bear.

SLITHER

Joy walked through the forest toward the clearing where he and Kinti had arrived earlier. While he walked, Joy held the shiny blue stone in his paw.

"I'm telling you Kinti, it was scary, but I wasn't scared. I'm not sure if that makes any sense," Joy said, "but that's the best way I can describe it."

Kinti hummed and whistled.

"And then there was that human that helped me. He didn't have to, but he did. He even said sorry for cutting down the forest. I thought the humans were all bad for what they did," Joy said. "I even thought maybe Keliru was right about the curse. But, seeing one up close, they weren't that scary. They are just trying to live too. Maybe they just don't understand how to respect Mother Earth?"

Kinti shrugged.

"Yeah, I don't know either. I wish I knew how the stone did what it did."

Joy put the stone back in the bag that hung from his shoulder and kept walking. From behind him, he heard voices. Human voices.

"The sun bear went this way!" one voice yelled out.

"Hurry! We have to catch him and cook him and eat him. His fur will make a nice rug!"

Joy looked at Kinti, "Oh no! Some of the humans must have followed us. Hurry Kinti, get up into the tree."

Joy climbed up the closest tree, all the way to the top branches. There, in the bottom of the canopy, he felt safely hidden among the thick leaves and vines. He took deep breaths and looked around for humans, but could not see any. He reached into his bag and grabbed the shiny blue stone.

"I know how I can find them," he said. He held the stone tightly in his paw and squeezed his eyes shut.

Nothing happened. Joy opened his eyes and shut them again, even more tightly. Still nothing.

"I don't get it, that's what happened before," Joy said. He opened the flap to the bag and looked inside. The stone wasn't glowing, and it wasn't warm.

"Strange," Joy said, "it must be sleepy."

Kinti suddenly flew right up to Joy's face buzzing and flitting excitedly.

"Whoa, Kinti," Joy said, "what is it?"

Kinti stopped flapping just long enough to point with one wing behind Joy. He turned to look and saw a giant brown python, as long as some trees were tall, staring right at him. It's giant, leaf-shaped head had a dark forked tongue that poked out and zipped back in. The python had strange dark circles around its eyes. It approached Joy quickly.

"Yikes!" Joy yelled, he scrambled out onto a branch, but with nowhere else to go, the snake had him trapped. The python crept around the trunk of the tree. "Kinti, hide!" Joy yelled.

The hummingbird dashed away, flying around another tree. Joy looked around for a way to escape. There were no branches close enough for him to jump to and change trees. He saw a vine draped over the branch he sat on and realized he had only one option. The python slithered out onto the branch and moved quickly.

The little sun bear grabbed the vine and jumped off the branch. The python snapped at him, but missed. Joy fell, feeling like he'd left his stomach up in the tree until the vine went tight. He swung in a long arc. When he reached as far as the vine would swing, he let go and grabbed the next one.

As he swung for a second time, Joy couldn't help but laugh. "It worked! It worked!" He looked up to see which tree the vine came from. When he looked up, he saw the python was suddenly in the tree above him. Joy could swear he saw the python smile, then it bit the vine Joy was holding onto.

Joy sailed through the air, landed on the ground and rolled a few times. He hit his nose on something and his eyes got watery. He rubbed them with his paws. He could hear the snake winding down the tree.

The python reached the ground and slithered forward. Joy backed up slowly, until he stumbled over a branch the size of his arm and fell on his back. The giant snake loomed over him, hissing loudly and opening its jaws wide enough to swallow Joy whole.

A high pitched whistle pierced the air. The snake paused, closing its mouth and looking up. A bright golden streak of light smacked the python across the face. The light zipped around a few trees and came back again, slapping the beast on the other side of its face, too.

The golden streak stopped and Joy saw it was Kinti. She flapped her wings and glowed brightly and charged at the python again.

But the python was ready this time. It opened its mouth and snatched Kinti right out of the air. The snake's head jerked left and right, up and down, as Kinti struggled to get out.

"No!" Joy yelled. "I can't lose you!"

SHIFTING

Joy got up and scratched with his long claws at the snake's belly. But the python's scales were too thick, and Joy couldn't hurt him. The snake's head continued flailing this way and that as Kinti fought inside its deadly jaws. The python heaved forward, knocking Joy back down to the ground. There, Joy's paw felt the branch he had tripped on a moment ago.

Joy grabbed the branch with both paws. Swinging it all the way around, he slammed it right into the side of the snake's head with a "CRACK!" The snake's mouth opened and Kinti flew out. The snake recoiled, then slithered off into the bushes.

Joy and Kinti didn't wait around. He grabbed the bag and they took off toward the clearing where they'd landed. As they approached it, Joy called out, "Kinti, transform, hurry!"

Kinti flew ahead and morphed back into a balloon. Joy scrambled inside her basket. He collapsed in the corner as she floated up into the air. Between his panting, Joy let out short little laughs.

"Okay," Joy said, "I think I've had enough of almost dying for one day. Let's go home. Slowly please, I need a chance to catch my breath."

Kinti hummed and floated along.

"Thank you Kinti, for saving me from the snake. And for bringing me out here," Joy said. He reached into his bag, "I couldn't have found the stone without you."

Kinti whistled.

Then Joy yelped.

"The stone! It's not here!" Joy started crying. "It must have fallen out when I hit the ground."

Kinti warbled a question.

Joy couldn't stop his tears. He got up and looked back at the forest behind them. "No Kinti," he said, "we can't go back. Between the snake and the humans who were following us, it isn't safe. I'll have to find a way to fix my mistake and help Tipah without the stone."

Joy sat down and sobbed. "And I'll have to tell my friend how I let her down, again. And how she'll never see her favorite shiny stone, all because of me."

*   *   *

From out of the bush where the python had escaped, the Trickster appeared in the shape of a fennec fox. Nine tails waved behind him and he wobbled on two legs as he rubbed the side of his face with his paw.

"Oh, by Aries, that hurt!" the Trickster said. "I haven't taken a blow like that in decades."

The sparkle of a small blue object on the ground got his attention.

"And what do we have here?" the Trickster asked out loud to no one.

The Trickster bent over and picked up the blue stone. He rotated it slowly, hypnotized by the tiny brown clouds inside it.

"My plan to make him drop the stone worked," he said, rubbing the stone on the fur of his chest to clean off some dirt. "I just wish I hadn't been smacked around so much to do it. That certainly wasn't part of my genius plan."

He took another look at the stone. He poked it with a tiny claw here and there.

"Now, stone," the Trickster said, "How did that annoying sun bear start you up? I watched him the whole time, but I didn't see how he activated you. I've worked with dozens of magic objects in my life but I've never seen one as...simple...as you are."

After a few minutes of examining it, the Trickster gave up.

"Oh fine, never mind," he said.

The Trickster flipped the stone into the air straight above him. As the stone sailed up, the Trickster jumped into the air with a flip, turning into a falcon in a puff of dark shadow.

The Trickster caught the stone in one talon and flapped up above the canopy.

"I'll have plenty of time to figure out the stone later. Now it's time to get back and enjoy my masterpiece of mayhem at that giant fig tree."

The Trickster cleared the canopy and took off at full speed back to Big Fig.

*   *   *

Some time later, Joy and Kinti landed just a short walk from Big Fig. Joy, slumped in the corner of

Kinti's basket, let out a few more gentle sobs. He did not get up to climb out.

"What am I going to do now? Without the stone, I don't know how I'm supposed to help," Joy said to Kinti. "I guess Viracocha was wrong. I can't help anyone."

Kinti gave a low whistle and hum, then shook her basket gently back and forth.

"No," Joy said, crossing his arms and making his face stern. "I'm not getting out. I can't help anyone without the blue stone, and even if I tried I'd only end up making things worse. Just like before."

Kinti let out a loud warble and buzzed. Then, without warning, she morphed back into a hummingbird. Joy floated in midair for a split second before plopping on the ground on his furry bottom.

"Ouch! Hey Kinti, that wasn't nice." Joy whined.

The gold and red hummingbird flew down in front of Joy's face, flitting back and forth. She let out every sound Joy had heard her make yet, from warbles to hums, to whistles and buzzes. It all sounded disconnected, and not happy. When she finished, she hovered in place and stared at Joy.

Joy leaned back slightly, looking sideways at Kinti. He'd never had a hummingbird yell at him before.

"But...what am I supposed to do? Viracocha sent me to find what I need to help my friend, but I lost the stone. What can a little sun bear like me do to help all those animals?"

Kinti whistled and warbled, then spat out a buzz.

Joy sighed. He held his paws up in front of him. "Okay. I'll go. But I think this is a mistake." Joy crawled up onto his feet, rubbing his back side with a paw. "Did you have to drop me on my butt?"

Kinti closed her eyes and warbled softly, turned around, and slowly flew toward Big Fig. Joy picked up the bag and followed her, limping just a little until the soreness in his back side faded.

He'd nearly made it back to the Great Big Fig Tree when he noticed it wasn't as loud as before.

"Kinti," Joy said, "how long have we been gone? Kinti?"

Joy looked around but could not see Kinti at all. He couldn't even hear her.

"Brother!" Ayu called out. She ran up to him. "There you are; I've been looking all over for you. Where have you been? I've been worried about you. And why do you have a human bag?"

Seeing his sister was a surprise for Joy. He didn't know which question to answer first.

"Well, uh, I went...um..."

"Ugh, never mind, you can tell me later. Hurry back with me; Keliru is leading a vote. If it goes his way, the refugees will have to leave and find a different forest!" Ayu said.

Joy's heart sank. "No! We can't let that happen," he said. "We have to stall, to buy them time."

"How?" Ayu asked. "And before you answer, be sure to hide that bag. If Keliru sees a human thing here you're going to be in big trouble."

"The bag, that's it!" Joy said. He opened his bag and looked inside. He picked out one of the figs and smiled. "Let's go get Tipah. I have a plan..."

PLANS

When the Trickster returned to Big Fig, he transformed back into a fennec fox in a puff of dark, smoky shadow. He felt proud of himself, and danced across a limb of Big Fig with a giant, smug smile on his face.

He returned to his spot high in the Great Big Fig Tree. He laid down and stretched out, lounging and soaking up the negative energy of fear and discord below him. The animals were quieter now, talking in small groups. But, the Trickster's giant fennec fox ears allowed him to eavesdrop on them.

The refugees discussed what they would do if the locals kicked them out of the forest. Meanwhile, the orangutans and other animals had broken into small groups. They each talked about whether to send the refugees away or not.

The Trickster was only half paying attention to the discussions below him, though. As he lay on the branch, he looked at the shiny blue stone he held in his little paw. He turned it and looked at every side, losing himself in the various shades of deep blue. The brown, swirling shapes he saw inside the stone reminded him of clouds.

His stony daydreams popped suddenly when the strong voice of a young female sun bear split the air.

"Hey, everyone, listen up," the sun bear said, in a voice as sweet as honey. The Trickster rolled over and looked down. On the forest floor below, the female sun bear walked into a beam of sunlight that

shone through the canopy. The light fell on her like a spotlight. Behind her ear was a pink flower, and the Trickster noticed the flower's shape matched the bear's light fur patch. The Trickster learned long ago how to avoid attention, but this sun bear knew how to get it. Her voice seemed to command the forest itself.

The Trickster smiled, the sparkle of the sun bear's coat in the sunlight reflected in his eyes. To the Trickster, she moved in graceful slow motion. Her big, brown eyes captivated the Trickster. In his mind he recalled some of the most beautiful music he'd ever heard in his long, long life.

"Look what I found!" she shouted, thrusting out her paw and showing everyone a big, ripe, fig.

The music in his imagination suddenly stopped. The Trickster's ears fell flat against his head. Shock widened his eyes and his jaw dropped.

"No! Where did she find that?" he hissed.

From another side of the gathering, the other young sun bear, the male, spoke up. "I found one too!" He held up another fig.

"That's impossible," the Trickster said to himself. "My illusion connects all the figs from this tree. That's why it took me all night to craft it!"

"Hey, me too," came a tiny little voice. From the group of refugees the little orangutan stepped into view, holding up another fig.

The big, grouchy orangutan looked back and forth between the three little animals. His mouth was wide

open in surprise. "Where did you find those?" he
growled.

"Yes, where?" the Trickster asked in a whisper. He
looked at Joy, "What are you up to, Joy?"

"Well, uh, we found them, that's what matters,"
Joy said. "And maybe, if everyone works together and
looks, we'll find more."

The Trickster ground his teeth and flicked his tail
nervously. The sun bear with the flower in her hair
spoke up again.

"Well, well, well," she said, wearing a smug smile. "Looks like my brother and Tipah, one of the refugees by the way, have found more figs than all your talk of curses did all morning. What are you waiting for? This proves there's no curse, the figs are here somewhere. Start looking!"

"No. no, no, no!" the Trickster growled. He looked up in the giant fig tree. He could see the web of magic that shaped his illusion beginning to break. He watched strings of the magic dim, then snap like a thin vine holding too much weight.

"My masterpiece!" he cried. He looked down below and saw several animals beginning to look around. They moved shrubs, sniffed under logs, and dug around roots. The Trickster knew they wouldn't find anything. However, the spell was falling apart, which meant that the animals below were beginning to question what was going on.

The Trickster held up both paws, squeezed his eyes shut and gritted his teeth. He struggled to weave his magic back together, but his illusion was too big and complex. It unraveled faster than he could fix it.

Panting from the effort of trying to fix his illusion, the Trickster wiped beads of sweat from his head with the paw that held the stone. His eyes popped open when he saw it.

"The stone," he said, fixing his face to look as in charge as he could, "you beautiful little piece of... of whatever you are. Give me your magic!"

But nothing happened. The Trickster's face went from in charge to in trouble. "Please? With your power I should be able to fix this elegant piece of magical artwork I made."

The Trickster shook the stone. He tapped it. Nothing happened.

He stuck his eye right on it, but saw no magic.

He held it out at straight in front of him, gritted his teeth and squinted, tightening every muscle he could think of. Still, no magic.

The Trickster growled. He blinked to the ground, hidden in the middle some bushes. He put the stone down, held himself up with his tails, put his paws on his knees, and tried meditating. The blue stone just laid still on the forest floor.

"Argh!" The Trickster yanked on his ears in frustration. He grabbed the stone and blew on it.

He chewed on it.

He rubbed it under his arm.

He banged it on his head.

He jumped on it.

He even kissed it and whispered to it how pretty it was.

"No magic?" The Trickster whined. "Not a spark. Not a glimmer!" He held the stone in the air and screamed, "Why won't you work?"

The Trickster peaked around the giant fig tree and looked at Joy.

"The sun bear. Something about him must activate the stone. I need him to start it, then I can steal it and use it. I'll have to be careful not to give myself away, but how—"

An evil grin stretched across the Trickster's snout and the tips of his ears rubbed together. "I have just the trick in mind," he said, then disappeared in a puff of dark shadow.

FRIENDS

Once all the animals were busy looking around for figs, Ayu, Tipah, and Joy met together. Under a nearby tree, off to the side of the commotion, the friends got together.

"Joy," Ayu said, "that worked, but it's not going to last long."

"Yeah," said Tipah, frowning, "it was clever, but I'm still scared. If they don't find any figs they're really going to believe in the curse this time."

Joy felt a lump in his throat. "You're both right. I think we bought a little time, but that's all. I'm really sorry Tipah"

"What are you sorry for, Joy?" Tipah asked. "You didn't do anything but try to help us."

Joy rubbed his paws together and looked down. "I saw your old home, and saw what you had to run from. I have a lot of respect for you, Tipah. You've still been kind and friendly, even after the world changed so much for you. I-I..."

Joy felt a bit choked up. Tipah reached over and put a hand on his shoulder. He looked over at her, and her big smile, and he felt the lump in his throat get softer.

"I had a chance to at least bring your favorite shiny thing back to you. But on my way back I lost it running from a giant snake. Now I think it's lost forever, and it's my fault. I'm sorry Tipah," Joy said.

Tipah stared at Joy in wonder. "You went all the way back to my home? And you tried to bring back my favorite shiny thing?" Tipah's eyes welled with tears. She gave Joy a big hug. "Thank you for even trying! That's the nicest thing any friend has done for me."

"How did you get there and back? That's a day's walk, at least," Ayu asked.

Joy didn't know what to say, but he knew his sister would know if he was lying. "I'll explain later. It doesn't matter though, it didn't work. I can't believe I almost had it. It was very special, pretty and blue, I can see why you liked it Tipah."

"Did you meet a squirrel while you were there?" Ayu asked.

Joy looked puzzled, "Yeah, how did you know?"

Ayu pointed behind Joy, "Because that one is holding something blue and pretty."

Joy turned around and saw a squirrel hopping out of a bush. The squirrel's fur was black on top and he had a reddish brown tummy, just like the little baby

133

squirrel Joy helped earlier. In his paws he held up the shiny blue stone.

"The stone!" Joy shouted. Tipah finally let go of Joy and smiled. Joy ran over to the squirrel and took the stone from the squirrel.

"Thank you!" Joy said. "Did you bring this all the way here for me?"

The little squirrel looked proud and chittered happily.

"Did you do this because I helped the little one?" Joy asked.

Again the squirrel made happy sounds, flicking his tail and nodding.

"How fast were you running? That's a long way to carry this," Joy said.

The squirrel paused for a moment, looking a bit surprised, then loudly gasped. He fell over onto his back and took deep, labored breaths.

"Well thank you. It means a lot to us," Joy said. He turned to Tipah and held out the blue stone. "Here Tipah, this is yours. If you have to leave, I'm glad you'll at least be able to take this with you."

The squirrel rolled over onto his tummy, reached out with a tiny paw and shook his head. He chittered nervously.

Tipah took the stone in her hand. Holding it up to the light, she admired how much it shined. "My favorite thing about this is how you can see into it. There's this magical world inside it, and there's always something new to find." Tipah placed the stone in Joy's paw. She closed his paw around the stone. "You keep it, Joy."

The squirrel sighed in relief.

Joy looked at Tipah with wide eyes. "But, it's your favorite thing."

"That's why I want you to have it, a thank you gift for all the kindness and respect you show the refugees. And me," Tipah said with a smile.

Joy smiled through tears and hugged Tipah. She hugged him back, squishing her face in his fur.

"Joy," Tipah said, her voice muffled by Joy's thick sun bear fur, "You're warm."

"Hugs are supposed to be warm," Joy said.

"No, you're really warm," Tipah said, then she let go and backed up, her face lit up with surprise. "Joy, you're glowing!"

Ayu, Tipah, and Joy stared at his heart patch which glowed brightly, just like the blue stone in his paw did. The squirrel rubbed his little paws together and stood up.

Ayu's eyes went wide and her mouth fell open. "What is going on Joy?" Ayu asked.

"It's doing it again!" Joy said. He shut his eyes tightly and felt his mind float out of his body. Floating outside his body, Joy looked around at Tipah, Ayu, and all the other animals around Big Fig.

"Whoa," Joy said. Everything was colorless, like before, and wrapped around Big Fig was a web of dark lines. Joy floated closer to the tree. All the animals, bugs, and leaves hung in the air, frozen in time. But when Joy looked closer, the dark web seemed to be vibrating. Tracing the lines of the web with his eyes, Joy could see that they connected to the ends of all the branches, roots, and—

"Figs!" Joy shouted. The shout echoed in that strange way again. "There are figs in the Great Big Fig Tree!" Joy floated all around the tree, taking the time to follow the dark lines of the web to its center. He could see that all the lines converged in one place, a fig at the very end of a branch high up in the tree.

Joy felt the familiar pull as the magic brought his mind back into his body. It didn't bother him

136

though, now that he knew what he needed to do. As his mind floated back into his body, he caught a glimpse of the squirrel behind him. The squirrel was frozen in time, running straight for Joy with his hands outstretched and a nervous expression on his face. For just a moment, he thought he saw a strange shadow surrounding the little creature.

Joy opened his eyes to find himself back in his body. To his surprise, he could still see the figs in the tree. They appeared as thin, transparent images, like reflections in the water. He looked back at the squirrel, looking carefully at him. He looked like an ordinary squirrel.

The squirrel stopped suddenly and looked back at Joy. He pulled his arms back and put them behind him, then smiled a toothy smile at Joy and waved a little paw.

"Huh," Joy said, then turned back to his sister and friend. "Ayu, Tipah, you're not going to believe this! There are figs in the Great Big Fig Tree, you just can't see them."

The squirrel behind him started chewing nervously on his tiny claws.

"What?" both Tipah and Ayu said at the same time.

"Trust me. I have to get up into Big Fig," Joy said.

Tipah smiled at Ayu, "He's glowing; I think we should believe him."

Ayu shook her head, "Keliru and the orangutans will never let you up there. They're the only animals not looking for figs. Instead, they're all guarding Big Fig."

Tipah smiled, "I have an idea that will get them out of the way."

THEATER

Joy, Ayu, Tipah, and the squirrel huddled close together under the tree where the refugees had rested earlier. The tree was old and covered in mushrooms. Behind the tree a dying corpse flower gave off the last of its strong stink. Around them the other animals murmured. They were starting to doubt that there were any more figs around.

"Joy, we don't have much time," Ayu said. "If every animal figures out it was a trick, they're going to let Keliru pass judgment. His word will be final, no one will argue."

"And all the refugees, and Tipah, will have to leave. I know. I have to get up into Big Fig," Joy said.

"What's your plan, Tipah?" Joy asked. His heart patch was still glowing, and so was the stone.

"This!" Tipah said, and she jumped into a patch of wet dirt and rolled around. Joy and Ayu looked at each other and frowned.

Tipah stood up, covered in bits of mud and stray leaves. She grabbed twigs from the ground and squeezed them in her armpits. Tucking a few mushrooms into her head, she turned to Joy and grinned.

"The apes are so afraid of a curse," Tipah said with a smile, "if we show them one they'll scatter like shrew mice."

"That's brilliant!" Joy said.

"It really is," said Ayu. Tipah and Joy looked at Ayu. "Oh, what, me too?"

"It'll be more believable," Tipah said.

Joy gave his sister his best little cub eyes, "Please sis?"

Ayu rolled her eyes, "I can't believe I'm doing this. Fine." She took out her pink flower and handed it to the squirrel. "Here, can you hold this please?"

The squirrel smiled dreamily and took the flower. It was nearly as big as he was, and he stuck his little face into it and drew in a deep breath through. The flower's sweet smell was intoxicating. The Trickster sat down and just stared at Ayu with a giant smile on his face.

Ayu didn't notice the squirrel's odd behavior. She walked over to the tree with the mushrooms.

"Aha, this will work," she said, plucking a handful of mushrooms. She arranged them in her hair and turned to her brother. "How do I look?"

Joy held back a laugh, snorting a little instead. "Cursed."

"You look great! But we need the finishing touch," Tipah said.

"What's that?" Ayu asked.

Tipah dropped the twigs she was holding and ran behind the tree. She came back with one of the large petals of the dying corpse flower.

"This!" Tipah said.

"Oh no, what are you doing with that?" asked Ayu.

Without answering, Tipah rubbed the petal all over herself. Then she turned and smiled at Ayu.

"No, no way," Ayu said, "not a corpse flower, I will not—"

Joy stared up at his sister with giant brown eyes.

"Cheater," said Ayu. "Fine. Give me that, please." Ayu carefully rubbed the flower on her fur, holding her breath as she did. "Oh, this is so gross!"

Tipah picked up her sticks and put them back under her arms. Ayu finished and tossed the petal into a bush.

"As soon as they're out of the way," Ayu said to Joy, "you run for it."

"I will," Joy said.

"Joy," Tipah said, "what about your glowing patch of fur and the stone?"

Joy walked over to the bush where he'd hidden the bag. He put the stone inside, then stashed the bag back in the bush. He walked past the squirrel, who was still smelling the flower with a big grin on his face. Joy went to the dirt Tipah had rolled in and scooped up a paw full. He rubbed it on his heart patch.

"It doesn't hide it completely, but it will have to do."

Ayu looked at Tipah. "Let's go," she said.

Tipah nodded, and together they approached the Great Big Fig Tree. Tipah went ahead first.

"Follow my lead," she said to Ayu. Ayu nodded carefully so that her mushrooms didn't fall out.

Tipah walked up to Keliru who was talking to another orangutan quietly. The orangutans smelled the stink in the air, then turned to see her. They stopped talking and leaned back away from the smell.

"What do you want, newcomer?" Keliru grumbled. He sniffed the air and flinched. "And why are you so filthy?"

"The curse!" Tipah said dramatically. She wobbled back and forth, twitching her arms like she was losing control of her body. "It's...taking...over...me... blaaggghh." Tipah moaned random sounds, talking like her tongue had swollen up.

Ayu could see how much fun Tipah was having. *Oh Tipah, Don't overdo it!* Ayu thought to herself.

But the thrill of performing distracted Tipah. As she stumbled around she paid no attention to where she stepped. Her toes caught on a root and she fell face down onto the ground.

Keliru and the other orangutan recoiled, but didn't move. Tipah's branches fell out from under her arms. Keliru looked closer, curious about the change. Ayu watched from a few feet away, nervously grinding her teeth. She took a deep breath and rushed forward.

Ayu walked up behind Tipah, stumbling around on two legs and holding her arms out in front of her. She rolled her eyes all the way up and moaned, "Mushrooms have grown out of my head! It's the curse, the curse, the cuuuuuurrrrrrrse." She let her long tongue roll out of her mouth and dangle as she walked.

That did it. The orangutans all yelped and scattered. Some ran to the other side of Big Fig while others fled to nearby trees.

Joy ran as fast as he could toward Big Fig. He ran between Ayu and Tipah, who were still acting cursed to keep the orangutans away. He got to the tree and leapt onto it. Using his long claws, he climbed as fast as he could.

The squirrel heard Joy run off and snapped out of his stupor. He turned and saw Joy climbing Big Fig. The winding roots made it easy for the sun bear to get up the tree. The Trickster squeaked, dropped the flower, and began looking around for the stone.

It has to be here somewhere, he thought. The sun bear doesn't have it in his claws; he's climbing. Where did he put it?

Joy made it to the first set of branches, but the branch with the fig he was looking for was still higher up.

The Trickster spotted the glow from the blue stone shining out of the satchel in a bush.

Joy got to the next big branch. One more to go, he thought.

The Trickster ran to the bush that hid the bag. Joy had pushed the bag into the bush, so as a squirrel, he couldn't reach it. He looked around to see if he was alone, and when he was sure it was safe, he transformed back into a fennec fox.

Joy reached the branch he was looking for. He climbed out onto it and looked around. He could still see faint images of the figs, but they were fading. Joy glanced down at his heart-patch, scraping away some of the dirt that covered it. The glow was fading too, and it was getting cooler.

The Trickster pulled on the strap of the bag. The thick branches of the bush caught on the bag and wouldn't let it out. He kept pulling.

Joy reached out and grabbed the fig at the end of the branch. In his paw he held the plump fruit as it faded more and more from his sight. His chance to save the refugees was almost gone.

REVEALED

W hat do I do with it?" he asked out loud. He heard a familiar buzzing sound and looked up. Kinti hovered above him in the trees.

"Kinti, there you are! I found what's hiding all the figs, some giant dark web that all comes from the fig that I'm holding. But what do I do with it?"

Kinti landed on the branch in front of Joy and opened her little beak, pointing into it with a wing tip.

Joy frowned at Kinti, "I don't think you can eat this whole thing Kinti. It's almost as big as you are."

Kinti frowned and covered her face with her wing.

Meanwhile, the Trickster yanked harder on the satchel, pulling it free from the bush. He opened the bag, licked his lips, and reached inside.

Kinti pointed at Joy, then pointed into her beak again.

"Oh, you want me to eat it?" Joy asked.

The little hummingbird nodded. "Well," Joy said, "I never say no to a snack."

The Trickster felt something warm, grabbed it, and pulled it from the bag. In his hand he could see the shiny blue stone. Inside the stone, all the cloudy brown shapes were glowing a brilliant gold.

"Yes!" the Trickster shouted. He held up the stone and danced in a circle. He ended his spin facing Big Fig. With a toothy grin, he lifted his paw and waved a hand at his illusion.

"I can feel the power," the Trickster said. "If I can just figure out how to channel it, I can—"

Joy popped the ghostly fig into his mouth and bit down on it. His fur tingled everywhere and he felt a blast of magical energy explode out from his body. The shock wave shattered the illusion as it grew, making a sound that only magical creatures could hear.

The wave of magical energy knocked Kinti off the branch and up into the air. She spun head over tail feathers, but flew into the blast to keep from blowing away. The wave continued to spread, passing harmlessly over the plants and animals of the forest.

The Trickster saw his illusion fall apart as the wall of magic expanded. Still holding the stone in the air, his ears went flat against his head and he frowned.

"Drat," whimpered the Trickster. The magic explosion smacked into him like a tidal wave, flinging him up into the air and far, far away across the forest.

The blue stone, unaffected by the wave of magic, dropped to the ground next to the satchel. All the animals stared in awe as figs appeared out of nowhere all over the Great Big Fig Tree.

Joy winked at Kinti, then carefully climbed down the tree. He walked over to Ayu and Tipah, who were looking up into the tree like everyone else. Joy looked down at his heart patch and saw it was no longer glowing.

"Joy, you were right," Ayu said. Her eyes were still wide and looking at all the figs that had just appeared.

"Where did they come from?" Tipah asked.

Keliru quickly stepped out from behind the Great Big Fig Tree, nearly tripping on a root. Another orangutan caught him, but he growled and pushed the helpful ape away. Keliru raised his hands and said loudly to all the animals, "It is as the Great Big Fig Tree said it would be. By looking for figs with the animals of this forest, the refugees have proven themselves worthy of being here. To welcome them, the Great Big Fig Tree has revealed his figs to us all. It is a miracle! Let the Harvest Day commence!"

Ayu turned to Joy and Tipah, crossed her arms and huffed, "Pfft, how does that overfed ape know Big Fig is a 'he'?"

Tipah and Joy giggled.

"Why does he get to take the credit?" Tipah asked.

"Yeah," Ayu said, tearing mushrooms from her head. "Good point, Tipah. As soon as I get these mushrooms all off my head I'm going to say something."

Joy ran around in front of Ayu and held his paws up. "Please don't sis. You and Tipah are right, he doesn't deserve any credit. But until I learn more about how I could see the figs, I think it's better if we keep our part quiet. I don't want to scare anyone, and I don't want them asking me questions."

Ayu looked at Joy and pointed a claw at him. "Fine. I have to go wash this stink out of my fur anyway. But you, little brother, have some serious explaining to do."

"I will sis. Just, not right now around all these other animals, okay?"

Ayu started to protest, but Tipah jumped in and said, "It's okay Joy. You can tell us when you're ready to. You've done so much today for all of us."

"We've done so much," said Joy. "I wouldn't have been able to do all that without both of you."

Ayu smiled, "Yeah, we did make a pretty good team."

Tipah's mother walked up to the trio of young animals. Tipah smiled, running up to give her a hug. "Mama!" she said.

"Good news, Tipah," the mother ape said, "there is a tree nearby that no one is using. Some of the local

150

orangutans have asked us to stay here, and said we could use it."

"Will it be... home?" Tipah asked, looking up at her mother with wide eyes.

"Yes, Tipah," said her mother, "this will be our new home."

Tipah smiled at Joy and Ayu, and the friends danced around to celebrate.

Joy heard Kinti faintly humming behind him in the forest. "I'll meet you at home Ayu, I've got to go take care of something. I'm glad you're staying Tipah. Let's play tomorrow."

"Okay!" Tipah said.

Joy waved goodbye and ran toward the bush where he'd left his new bag. Along the way he found Ayu's flower and picked it up. He looked around for the squirrel, but could not find him. To his surprise, the satchel wasn't in the bush, but in front of it, with the shiny blue stone next to it.

Joy collected the stone and put it, and the flower, into the bag. Throwing the strap over his shoulder, he ran off into the forest. After a little walk, Kinti joined him, and they trekked silently toward the Dark Forest.

It didn't take long before they found the pond where Joy had met Viracocha. Joy approached slowly, looking for any sign of the tiger that had attacked him earlier that day.

"Kinti," Joy whispered, "can you see if the tiger lurks nearby?"

Kinti gave a tiny salute with her wing, zipped around the pond and back. She disappeared for a minute and Joy began to worry. But then she came back and gave Joy a smile and a happy warble. Together they walked to the pond.

Joy found Viracocha sitting on the same fern leaf as before, hanging over the water. The frog and the fern leaf were softly glowing, just like Kinti. Joy also noticed that he saw no reflection in the water of the leaf or the frog. So that's what looked strange about the leaf earlier, Joy thought.

"You're magical too, huh?" Joy asked.

"A little bit," Viracocha said with a smile. "Did you help your friend out?"

Joy smiled, "Yes, I did. And I wouldn't have been able to do it without the stone you sent me to find."

"Oh that," said Viracocha, "was only part of what you found..."

ANSWERS

Y ou're right," Joy said, taking the blue stone out of his bag, "I also found this really helpful bag. I do feel bad for taking it from the human without asking, though."

Viracocha waved his front feet back and forth, shaking his head. "No! That isn't what I mean. Sure, the bag is nice, but what did you find inside yourself?"

"Inside me? What do you mean?"

"Kinti already shared your adventure with me. Joy, you found the courage to stand up and help others. You found the bravery to go somewhere you'd never been. You found the strength to stand up to bigger, scarier animals and humans. And you found that special kind of respect for others that only comes from seeing where they've been."

Joy thought about that for a moment. "Whoa, you're right." Joy blew out a deep breath and leaned back on his paws. "This has been the biggest day of my life."

"So far."

"What was that?" Joy asked.

"What?" Viracocha said. Then changing the subject, "Joy, that blue amber you found, it's not just a shiny thing anymore. After the adventure you shared with it, it has something special inside."

"It's called blue amber?" Joy asked. He held up the stone and peered at the swirling, cloud-like shapes within it. In faint, ghostly images, he could see events he remembered from the day. "Whoa. How did that happen?"

Viracocha cleared his throat. "I can explain, but first, Joy, I need to show you something. And please, don't panic when I do."

"Why would I panic?" Joy asked, looking up from the stone.

Instead of answering, Viracocha closed his eyes. The frog, and the fern leaf, glowed brightly, like Kinti did when she transformed. Joy covered his eyes until the light went away. When he looked up again he gasped.

"I-I can't believe my eyes," Joy said.

"It's okay Joy, this is just what I normally look like," said Viracocha. He had taken the form of a small, shiny golden being that looked something like a human, but not exactly. He was only a little taller than Papa Bear, with stocky limbs, a flat face, and eyes so dark they looked like little holes. On his head was a feathered headpiece, and he wore a tunic, a long shirt, and a belt. He also had an assortment of jewelry around his neck

154

and in his ears. If Joy looked carefully, he could see through Viracocha to the waterfall behind him.

"So, you're not a frog?" Joy asked.

Viracocha smiled and shook his head, "No, I'm afraid not. I apologize for the disguise earlier, but I did not want to scare you." Kinti flew up next to Viracocha and hovered there, smiling.

Joy rubbed his eyes. "Why can I see through you?" he asked.

"I'm not actually where you are Joy. What you're seeing right now is like a reflection. Similar to when you look in the water and see yourself, but you're not in the water. The frog was a different kind of reflection, and it was harder to make because I had to imagine what I wanted it to look like. Because of that, I can talk a little longer like this, my plain self."

Joy looked down at the water. He could see himself in the water, and Kinti, but no reflection of Viracocha. Just a soft glow on the surface of the pond. "Well if you're not here, where are you?" Joy picked a stick up off the ground.

Viracocha sighed. "That, little sun bear, is the problem. I, and many others like me, are stuck in—"

Joy waved the stick back and forth through Viracocha's transparent body. The stick passed right through without disturbing the image at all.

"Do you mind? I don't have all day to tell you this..."

Joy dropped the stick into the water and smiled, "just checking."

"Anyway, the others and I are in, well, you might call it the Spirit World."

Joy's mouth fell open. "So Keliru was right about the Spirit World?"

Viracocha waved a hand, "No, not even close. I'm just using that name because it makes sense to you. There have been a lot of names for it, but we'll stick with that."

"Why are you stuck there?" Joy asked.

"Remember when I said that I tried to help some animals a very long time ago?" Viracocha asked. "Well, those animals were the humans. The others and I went to Earth to try and teach them how to live in harmony with the planet. Sadly, we weren't able to teach them everything they needed to learn before we... Well, we had to leave."

Viracocha waved his hand in the air and an image of a giant stone sculpture appeared. Two rectangle stones held another that stretched across their tops. Tiny engravings of little winged beings, and an image of Viracocha, covered the top stone. Between the two bottom stones was a space, and Joy could see the sun setting in the distance.

"Our plan was to return, but something happened to our gate, the Gate of the Sun. Something damaged the gate on your end, on Earth. Now, we're all trapped here and unable to help finish what we started."

"That's terrible," Joy said.

"Now, I'm sorry to say, the humans know enough to grow and expand, but now they take from Mother Earth far more than they give."

"Is that why they cut down Tipah's home?" Joy asked.

Viracocha sighed, "Yes. They have a lot of greatness and beauty in them, but they can cause a lot of damage when they are careless. And there are so many groups of them. Every group has a unique culture, a way they live and think. There are so many different cultures out there that they don't always understand or respect each other. This causes a lot of confusion and carelessness. I think you can help though."

Joy pointed at himself with a claw, "Who, me? How in the world am I supposed to help all of Mother Earth?"

"Yes, you," Viracocha laughed. "You have a special gift, Joy. You have magic in you. That stone is just a pretty stone, but combined with your magic and compassion it's become something much more. It is a piece of a puzzle that will help Mother Earth and all who inhabit her."

Viracocha stared at Joy with the smile of a bear cub about to get his first fig. "You are the key, Joy!"

CHOICE

Joy frowned, shrugging his shoulders and holding his paws up. "The key to what?"

"Fixing the Gate of the Sun," answered Viracocha. "The damage to the gate exists on your side, but here in Spirit World it still stands. We built it from the lessons we wanted to give to humans. Respect was one of the first lessons the others and I had come to Earth to teach mankind.

"You see those images in the stone? Your magic combined with the stone when you acted with compassion and respect. Just like how respect helps you see ideas from another's perspective, the stone focused your magic to let you see things you can't with just your eyes."

Joy scrunched his nose and raised an eyebrow. "So, when I could see things from outside myself..."

Viracocha chimed in, "The magic in you was using the essence of respect. Now that essence is in the blue amber. If you take the blue amber to the Gate of the Sun, we might be able to repair part of it."

"Only part of it?"

"There are many lessons we wanted to share. You will have to find them all throughout the world by traveling, learning about humans, and collecting more stones. If you can learn them and imbue the stones with their essence, like you did with this blue amber, then we may be able to fix all of it. And who knows what kinds of interesting tricks you'll learn in the process? Then the gate will let the others and I back through, and we can finish teaching the humans what they need to learn. Do you think you can do that?"

Joy's heart raced and his head spun. The idea of helping the whole world was more than he could understand.

"It felt good to help Tipah and the refugees," Joy said. "But that was hard, and scary, and dangerous. Helping the whole world would be..."

Viracocha's smile faded, and he spoke in a serious tone and said, "All that. And probably more."

Joy looked up at Viracocha. "What if I say no?" Joy asked.

Viracocha shrugged. "Then nothing changes. The world continues going the way it is. Humans continue taking whatever they think they need. Or whatever they want."

"They'll cut down more forests?" Joy asked.

Viracocha nodded. "Probably. Until there aren't any left, of course. I know it's a big request. You'll have

Kinti, and the help of all the others and I, however we can. But the choice is yours."

Joy thought about what Tipah and the refugees had gone through after their forest was cut down. He thought about that nice human who hadn't wanted to cut it down. He thought about his family, and how he wouldn't want them to suffer if the humans came for their forest.

"If that's what it will take to help protect my forest, then I'll do it." Joy said.

Kinti trilled and flew in circles. Viracocha smiled. "I'm glad to hear it. But be cautious, Joy. I can't prove it, but I think a trickster hid the figs in your Great Big Fig Tree with an illusion."

"What's a trickster?" Joy asked.

"A magical creature that can take different shapes. They feed off sadness, chaos, and negativity. They can hide their magic, and they can't stand being recognized. It will probably run away now that you broke the illusion. But it might return, so you need to be vigilant, and be sure that whoever you talk to is someone you can trust."

Joy took a deep breath. His heart still raced, but he looked at the blue amber in his paw and he felt calmer. "Well, what do we do next?" he asked.

"For now, go home little bear," Viracocha said. "Get some rest. It's been a very big day for you. Kinti will find you and let you know when I figure out where you need to go next. Then, she'll take you there. My time is up, for now. I can only project my image to you for a little while, and only over water. Take care, Joy, and thank you."

Viracocha faded from view, and through his thinning image Kinti flew right into Joy's heart patch. She smiled and gave him a hug with her tiny wings. Joy laughed and gently hugged her back. It was starting to get dark, so Joy got up, put the stone back in the satchel, and headed home.

"Kinti, can you help light the way?" Joy asked.

Kinti flew ahead of him slowly, glowing softly and lighting the forest in her warm, golden glow.

*   *   *

The white cockatoo with bright yellow feathers on his head stretched out his wings and yawned. He'd been flying for most of the day to get as far away from the creepy, shape-shifting creature that had terrified him earlier.

He looked around one more time. The tree he perched in sat next to a tiny stream, and the trickling water was relaxing. When he was sure that no predators were nearby, he sighed, and let his eyes droop shut.

Meanwhile, the Trickster sailed over the forest after the magic blast wave smacked him into the air. When his spell fell apart, the uncontrolled energy of the illusion exploded outward. Being a magical creature, he felt the shock wave while normal creatures didn't.

The Trickster howled as he began falling back to Earth. He crashed through the canopy, sending leaves this way and that. Branch after branch snapped under his momentum, until he crashed into the tree limb that the cockatoo now slept on.

The cockatoo squawked in surprise, losing yet another dozen feathers. He held up his wings shield his face from flying pieces of branch. Looking carefully over his wing, the cockatoo squawked again and backed up.

Laying hung over the tree limb was a fennec fox with nine tails. The Trickster lay there like a limp vine for a moment, then looked up slowly. One eye was puffy and his fur messy and full of bark and leaves. When he saw the cockatoo, the Trickster smiled and showed a few missing teeth.

"My, friend," he said weakly. "I'm so glad you're here."

The cockatoo squawked, shook his head, and took off. He flew away as fast as his wings could take him.

"Wait!" said the Trickster, but the limb that held him finally gave way, and the fox fell the rest of the way to into the stream.

The water flowed around the Trickster, who slowly crawled out of the stream onto the dirt beside it.

"I just wanted to talk to someone," whined the Trickster.

From behind the Trickster, a dark cloud appeared over the stream. Inside the cloud, two red eyes fixed themselves on the Trickster.

"You can talk to me," said a dark, menacing voice from within the cloud.

The Trickster's ears went flat and his throat tightened up. He slowly turned around, smiled nervously at the eyes, and gave a tiny wave of his paw. "Oh, hi boss."

"It's been a long time," said the voice in the cloud. "We have some catching up to do."

"Yeah, sure," the Trickster avoided looking directly at the cloud.

"And, since you bungled the last job I gave you so many years ago, I have a new task for you," the voice said. The eyes narrowed to slits and aimed straight at the Trickster.

"Uh, of course boss, whatever you ask you know I'll do it."

"Let's see if you can get it right this time," the voice seemed to drip disappointment.

GOODNIGHT

Joy and Kinti made it home safely, even with nighttime arriving and making everything darker. He took Ayu's pink flower out of the bag. With the blue amber inside, he hid the bag in a hollow space in the trunk of his tree. Grabbing some branches and fern leaves, Joy covered the space to conceal the backpack. Kinti perched on Joy's shoulder.

"Kinti," Joy said, "this is huge. I'm not sure how I'm supposed to do this. And what do I tell Mama and Papa? That some fantastical frog helped me break the magic that hid the figs, then turned into a glowing gold-man who wasn't really there and asked me to travel the world in a hummingbird that turns into a red air balloon? That's crazy! Am I crazy?" Joy panted.

The hummingbird shrugged. The bushes nearby rustled. Joy crouched, ready to run. Kinti flew off his shoulder, glowing brightly so they could see.

Ayu jumped out of the bushes. "Aha!" She exclaimed. "I knew you were hiding something!"

"Ayu!" Joy relaxed a bit and Kinti flew behind him, glowing as little as she could. Joy worried that his big sister had seen Kinti. "Uh, how long have you been there?"

Ayu sauntered over to Joy, poking his chest with a claw. "Long enough to hear you conveniently explain

everything. And why is there a glowing bird with you? And how come you get to talk to some magic frog, huh? Did he give you the stone that made you glow?"

"Uh, er..." Joy stammered. Kinti poked her head up over Joy's shoulder, smiling a little at Ayu. Joy remembered Viracocha's warning about a Trickster. "Hey!" Joy scowled at his sister, "how do I know you're really Ayu?"

Ayu put her paws on her hips and leaned forward, putting her nose right up against Joy's and exhaled through clenched teeth. "Listen, fig brain, I'll ask the questions here. I'm the big sister, remember?"

Joy smiled meekly, "Yup, you're you. Ayu, meet Kinti. She's a new friend, and a very special bird." Joy held up Ayu's flower. "Here, I saved this for you."

Ayu's expression softened as she took the flower. "Thank you, I thought that shifty little squirrel had stolen it." She looked up at Joy, frowning. "Little brother, what did you get yourself into?"

"It's complicated," Joy said.

Joy gave his sister as short a story as he could. "... And now, Viracocha needs me to travel the world with Kinti, to get the rest of the lessons and stones needed to fix the Gate of the Sun. If I don't, it may only be a matter of time before the humans come to our forest too."

Ayu frowned. "Can I convince you not to do this?"

Joy looked at Kinti, then back at Ayu. "I don't think so."

Ayu sighed. "Fine. Then I'm coming with you. And don't even think about saying 'no.'"

"Okay," Joy said, smiling. "I'd like that."

"There's no way Mama and Papa will let you go, though. You'll have to figure out a really good way to tell them, or they're never going to let you out of their sight," Ayu said.

"That could take a while to figure out," Joy said, frowning. "I'll have to do that later. Not tonight, I'm tired."

Joy hugged his sister, then climbed up into his tree to find his nest.

Ayu stayed on the ground, looking at Kinti hovering in front of her. "Nice to meet you, Kinti."

Kinti smiled and gave Ayu a happy warble.

Ayu grinned. "Listen, there's no way he's going anywhere where I can't protect him again. Will you be sure to come get me if you two have to go somewhere?"

Kinti nodded, then with a stern expression, gave Ayu a tiny salute with her wing. She buzzed over and nuzzled her head against Ayu's cheek before flying up into the tree to meet Joy in his nest.

Ayu smiled and climbed up her tree.

Up in the tree, Joy said goodnight to Mama Sun Bear. Papa was already snoring in his nest, one leg dangling in mid air. Joy smiled, curled up in a ball, and fell asleep right away. His dreams were full of delicious food and great friends, open skies and music, and adventure and magic.

JOY SUN BEAR'S ADVENTURES WILL CONTINUE IN BOOK TWO! VISIT OUR WEBSITE TO STAY UP TO DATE ON HIS ADVENTURES AND ENJOY OTHER STORIES AND ACTIVITIES.

<u>Fiction Meets Informational Text</u>

To share the world with you, the reader, the authors have included several informational facts in the story. Lots of research was done on the wildlife and plant life of Sumatra to give you the opportunity to learn about the world while reading Joy's magical adventure.

Our website also provides a **free educational section** that features resources to teach children about Sumatra, and several other countries, in a kid-friendly way.

Kids will learn about geography, traditions, food, animals, plants, music and more, through Joy's perspective. The site also includes fun crafts, free coloring activities, videos, and recipes for children.

Visit our website to start your adventure!

www.joysunbear.com

Enjoy learning more about the world through our book and website and don't forget to "*See the World with Joy!*"

Share your thoughts and questions
with us at **info@joysunbear.com**

KIDS, DO YOU WANT TO LEARN HOW YOU CAN HELP REDUCE DEFORESTATION?

Interested in learning how you can keep rainforests in the world, like Sumatra, safe while helping animals like Joy and Tipah? Here are some ways you can help make a difference!

1. Plant a Tree - With the help of family, friends and neighbors, you can organize an event to plant trees in your community. Learning about how trees grow will help develop an appreciation for the process, and a healthy respect for our forests. More trees in your community will also give off oxygen, cool the area with shade, and filter harmful pollutants and dust from the air.

2. Reduce, Reuse and Recycle - Help with recycling at home and school and encourage your family and friends to get involved. Using less paper products means there will be a lower demand to cut down trees to make new products.

3. Reduce your Impact on the Environment - Ask your parents to buy foods that are grown in a sustainable way. *Sustainable* means that the process of growing it doesn't hurt the environment. There are many products provided by companies that are environmentally friendly.

4. Fundraise - Organize a fundraiser at school or put on a bake sale to raise money for organizations that help animals and rainforests. Often these organizations use extra money to purchase portions of rainforest to keep it safe.

5. Don't Waste Paper - Use both sides when you are writing and drawing and do your best to fill the page. Less paper used means that paper manufacturers won't have to make as much. This will result in less trees being cut down.

6. Reduce the Use of Palm Oil - You will find palm oil in many products like vegan butters, ice cream, baked goods and even cosmetics. Palm oil is grown on plantations; generally this means it is farmland that used to be rainforest, like Tipah's home in the story. Like paper, using less means less forests are being cut down to make room for palm oil manufacturing.

7. Treat Pencils Like Gold - Cherish them and don't waste them. Most pencil manufacturers are already using sustainable farming practices, but just like paper and palm oil, less demand means less trees being cut down.

8. Build Awareness about Deforestation - Ask your teacher if you can do a class project or play about helping rainforests. Teach others about the plants and animals in rainforests and why they are so important to the world. Share how others can help in their community and globally through different organizations.

You can work with your parents and teachers to help organizations that work to conserve rainforests and help the animals that live there, such as:

- **World Wildlife Fund (WWF) - (worldwildlife.org)**: Offers help to sustain food, climate, freshwater, wildlife, forests and oceans all around the world.
- **Free the Bears and Bornean Sun Bear Conservation Centre - (freethebears.org)**: Where you can sponsor or adopt sun bears like Joy to help out.
- **Rainforest Alliance - (rainforest-alliance.org)**: Where you can help the rainforest and its animals by donating and finding certified products that are better for you and the environment. Also has kids activities and games!

Remember, no matter how old you are or where you are from, you can make a positive difference in the world!

*Please remember to show respect to your parents, guardian and/or teacher and ask for permission before visiting any of the websites listed above.

HOW CAN YOU, YOUR FAMILY, AND CLASSROOM HELP REFUGEES?

Over 68.5 million people around the world are fleeing their homes like Tipah and the newcomers. Nearly 25.4 million of these people are refugees with over half of them being children.* These families do not wish to leave, but often have no choice due to events out of their control. Here are some ways you and your family can help:

1. **Show Respect and Kindness to Newcomers** - A new student or neighbor may or may not be a refugee, but they are still new to the school and community. Many kids who first start out in a new school are nervous that they will not make any new friends. Remember that if you were new and had to leave your old home, you would feel scared and alone too.

Even though it may feel weird to have someone new in your class, try welcoming the new student with respect and kindness, just like Joy and Ayu did in the story. You can show them care by asking them to sit with you at lunch or join your group to play at recess. Ask your teacher if you can work on a project together or see if they want to organize a play date. There are many ways to help newcomers feel welcome!

2. **Send a Letter of Hope to a Child** - Refugees are people just like you who have to leave their home unexpectedly. Send a kind letter to a child who has fled their home and show them that they are not alone. You and your parent/teacher can do so through an organization called **CARE**:
   my.care.org/site/SPageNavigator/CARE_SpecialDelivery.html

3. **Organize a Fundraiser to Donate Goods** - Ask your parent or school if you can have a fundraiser to collect household goods, school supplies, books, toys and furniture for refugees. You can donate your goods to the **International Rescue Committee**:
   rescue.org

174

4. Organize a Fundraiser to Donate Funds - Organize a lemonade stand or bake sale to raise funds to help refugees through organizations like **Save the Children, Global Giving, World Vision** or **Mercy-USA for Aid and Development** (links provided below):

- **savethechildren.org**
- **globalgiving.org**
- **worldvision.org**
- **mercyusa.org**

5. Help Out at Home or in your Community to Raise Funds - Let your family, friends and neighbors know that you want to help refugees by doing chores to raise funds. By taking some time each week, you can mow the lawn, fold laundry, or help clean out the garage to collect money to help provide refugees food, solar light, clothes, and a safe place to play and learn.

*Please remember to show respect to your parents, guardian and/or teacher and ask for permission before visiting any of the websites listed above.

Thank you for reading and helping the world with Joy!

* Statistics provided by www.unrefugees.org.

Blanca Carranza, Co-Author

Blanca Carranza is a former preschool teacher and globetrotter. Born in New York to Colombian parents, she spent her early life traveling around the world and listening to her grandmothers' stories. She has visited fifteen countries across four continents. Her passion for exploring the world, combined with her study of child development, created a unique atmosphere in each of the daycares and preschools she has owned and operated.

From international music, to food, to art, she brought the world to the children she cared for. Before retiring from childcare, she was inspired to create Joy Sun Bear and his adventures so she could continue to help children be happier and learn more about the world. She has two kids of her own, both all grown up, and lives in Southern California with her husband.

John Lee, Co-Author and Illustrator

From driving tanks in the U.S. Army, to problem solving in the IT world, to writing and drawing cute and cuddly animals on magical adventures, John's life has been fun and diverse.

Drawing and storytelling have always been important hobbies for John. Fueled by books, video games, and copious amounts of coffee, he is always excited to read, watch, or create some adventure-filled fiction.

John adores time with his wife and daughter, who provide a limitless supply of love, inspiration, and motivation. Together they live in sunny Southern California.